A Western Horseman book

TEAM PENNING

By Phil Livingston

Edited by Pat Close

Photographs by Charlie Carrel
and Pat Close

TEAM
PENNING

Published by
Western Horseman Inc.

3850 North Nevada Ave.
Box 7980
Colorado Springs, CO 80933-7980

Design, Typography, and Production
Western Horseman
Colorado Springs, Colorado

Printing
McCormick-Armstrong Co. Inc.
Colorado Springs, Colorado

Fourth Printing: June 1995

ISBN 0-911647-24-4

DEDICATION

This book is dedicated to team penners everywhere, individuals who participate and enjoy the sport regardless of what level. To those of you who thrill at the competition, enjoy the fellowship with other penners, and appreciate good horses, may all your runs be in the :30s.

Phil Livingston

PHIL LIVINGSTON

ACKNOWLEDGMENTS

A book like this just doesn't jump into print as the result of one person's effort. A lot of people have to contribute. In this case, friends banded together to provide facilities, the cattle, their time, and horses to demonstrate what team penning is all about, and gave freely in their advice and constructive criticism of the editorial copy. Without their help, this couldn't have been done. To all of you: *Muchas gracias, amigos mio.*

Mrs. Dawn McDavid, Weatherford, Tex.—for graciously allowing the use of the arena and other facilities on her Bull Goose Ranch for holding a private team penning where many of the photos in this book were shot.

Kenneth Danley, Weatherford, Tex.—for helping with this project as the manager of the Bull Goose Ranch and also as a long-time roping partner and friend to ride the river with.

Ted Scarbrough, Cresson, Tex.—for providing us with a fine set of cattle.

To the following for taking the time to bring their horses and spend two days penning with us while photographs were taken.

Kay Baker, Pete and Jo Bonds, C.R. and Sally Bridges, Lin Cozart, Jamie French, Pratt Phillips, Buck Thomas, Marvin Thomas, Jennifer Travis, Hill Stepp, and Bill Shisler, Publisher, *Team Penning U.S.A.* magazine.

Kitty (Mrs. Kenneth) Danley—for providing mighty fine lunches during the two days of team penning.

M.C. Baker, D.V.M., Weatherford, Tex.—for working out the charts in Chapter 8 regarding how cattle see—and react to riders.

Last, but certainly not least, my wife, Carol, who team penned during the two days, coordinated activities, ran errands, had coffee available, made sure everyone got fed, helped to proofread this book, and performed a herd of other chores to help make sure this book got into print.

One final note: Other photographs used in this book were taken at sanctioned team penning contests in Saginaw, Tex., and Las Vegas, Nevada.

—*Phil Livingston*

BASIC RULES

Every team penning association has its own set of rules, as does the American Quarter Horse Association for contests that it approves. The rules of all the associations are basically the same, but there can be variations. For example, some associations have a 90-second time limit instead of a 2-minute limit. Some contests also operate by their own rules, which might vary from standard rules. One example: After penning their cattle, the team must close the gate to the pen before calling for time.

Here is a basic set of rules; but before any penning contest, make sure you are familiar with the rules under which it will be judged.

1/ The working order for the go-rounds will be established by a random draw. But in the final go, in which only the 10 teams with the fastest times compete, the team with the highest time will work first, and the team with the lowest time will work last. If for any reason a team is not ready to compete when called, they will be disqualified.

2/ Within a 2-minute time limit, a team must separate from the herd three head of cattle which are identified alike and pen the cattle. A team must be given a 30-second warning.

3/ A team can pen one, two, or three head. However, three head penned always beats two head penned, and two head penned always beats one head penned.

4/ When a team begins a run, there will be 30 head of cattle bunched on the cattle side of the start/foul line. The flagman will raise the flag to signal when the team may begin and will drop the flag as the nose of the first horse crosses the start/foul line. When the flag is dropped, time will begin, and the team will be considered committed to the cattle.

5/ Teams will be given their cattle number when the flagman drops the flag.

6/ To call for time, after penning its cattle, one team member must ride through the gate with arm raised.

7/ In the event there are any unpenned cattle on the pen side of the start/foul line when time is called for, time will continue until all cattle are driven to the cattle side of the line.

8/ If at any one time more than four head of cattle cross the start/foul line, the team will be disqualified.

9/ If a team observes an unfit, injured, or unidentifiable animal after committing to the cattle, they must immediately pull up and notify the judge. In the event the judge rules the team is entitled to a rerun, they will be allowed to work at the conclusion of the go-round.

10/ In the event of a technical or mechanical error, the team will be given a rerun at the conclusion of the go-round.

11/ Contact with cattle by any equipment (hats, bats, ropes, reins, etc.) will result in the team's disqualification. No undue roughness will be tolerated, and a team will be disqualified should they exhibit any form of poor sportsmanship.

12/ All team members must be dressed in proper western attire upon crossing the start/foul line. This must include western shirt, cowboy hat, and boots.

13/ The decision of the judges will be final, and no disputes will be allowed.

CONTENTS

1 WHAT IS TEAM PENNING?

It has developed into a sport in which anyone who can ride a horse can participate.

DURING THE last decade, no event has taken over the horse world as has team penning. The appeal is universal, and people from all walks of life and from clear across the country are competing. Some stay in their own backyards, attending the small jackpots and practice sessions. Others have stepped out and made their mark at the "high-dollar contests" that are appearing.

No cowboy background is necessary to team pen. It doesn't require the specialized skills or the highly trained mounts that roping, reining, and cutting do. There is no discrimination because of age or sex, and it is a sport in which all members of a family can participate. In fact, members of the same family frequently compete together and make up one or more teams.

Your saddle doesn't have to sparkle with silver, and your horse can lack show-ring conformation and glow. No one cares if a rider hangs on to the saddle horn or cues his mount. All that matters is that you

The object of team penning is to cut out and pen your three head faster than any other team.

The designated cutter gallops toward the herd while his teammates stay back, waiting to see where they are needed. The rider on the far right is leaving the arena after settling the herd between runs.

The cutter splits part of the herd off to one side, looking for cows with the designated number.

and your teammates cut out and then drive your assigned three head of cattle into the pen faster than any other team.

Sometimes your efforts work like a charm and the cattle trot right down the arena in a group and swing around the wing into the pen. Other times, the herd resembles a covey of startled quail and

nothing works. But regardless of what happens during your run, team penning is FUN.

The sport began in California during the middle 1950s, when a number of ranch cowboys got together to make a contest out of separating and corralling cattle.

9

His teammates gallop over to turn back the wrong-numbered cattle.

Here's another team, in a different arena, that has its three head galloping toward the pen.

As the cattle approach the pen, the rider on the left automatically becomes the hole rider; the rider in the middle, the wing man; and the rider on the right, the swing man.

The swing man will stay behind the cattle, pushing them around the end of the arena toward the pen. The wing man will ride to the end of the wing, blocking the cattle from going back down the arena.

11

Here's another team that has successfully penned its three head.

A lot of team penners start young.

Instead of roping, riding broncs, or just cutting, they figured that sorting out a designated number of yearlings from the herd and then hazing them through a gate (as they did when they were actually sorting cattle on the ranch) would be a fun kind of contest. It was, and the sport gradually began to grow. Over the years formal rules were drawn up and the contest became more standardized. The number of cattle to be cut out and penned was experimented with, as was the number of contestants on a team and the time allowed for each team to pen their animals.

Finally, after lots of trial and error, it was decided that separating and penning three like-numbered animals from a herd of thirty was a good contest, and allowing a team of three riders 2 minutes to get the job done worked out just fine. More riders than three just got in each other's way.

Team penning was on the move and gradually spread north and east as more and more horsemen heard about it.

The rules for team penning are simple. Although there are some variations in different parts of the country, and between different associations, the basic idea is the same everywhere. A team of three riders, starting from behind a line, has 2 minutes to enter a herd of thirty cattle located at the far end of the arena. The object is to separate the three head

Waiting for the contest to start, team penners relax and visit with friends.

bearing the team's assigned number, drive them up the arena, and corral them in the small pen set off to one side.

Time stops when all three animals are penned and at least one contestant rides through the gate and raises his arm. It is possible for a team to receive time with only one or two head penned, but more credit is given if they pen three. And a team that pens three always places higher than a team that only pens two, regardless if the latter team has a faster time.

A team can be disqualified for having more than four head of cattle across the starting/foul line at one time, for signaling for time when an extra or incorrectly numbered animal is in the pen or for not driving it back across the foul line, and for striking or being unnecessarily rough on the cattle. The latter penalty is called at the discretion of one or both of the judges.

Knowledge of a few of the finer points of team penning can make the sport more enjoyable for spectators and contestants alike. Even if you don't ride, it is an event that can be appreciated from the stands, since it is easy to understand, fast, exciting, and a team's fortunes can change rapidly from a successful run to failure.

Watch the way team members work together, setting up the run, and reacting almost automatically as the action develops. Notice the understanding that many penners seem to have of how a cow

will react; they always position themselves to move the animal in the desired direction. And, of course, the cow sense that a good horse can demonstrate is always enjoyable to watch. All of this can take place within a single run, one that often stops the clock in under half a minute.

The roots of team penning are buried in the American West, back in the days when the trail herds were "shaped up" and sent north. It took a top hand mounted on a good horse to handle those wild Longhorn cattle and required that man and mount work as a team. Now, those skills have moved to the arena, just as other ranch work has, and have become a contest against time. It has developed into a sport, one in which anyone who can ride a horse can participate. And, besides the challenge of competition, team penning offers the opportunity to be outdoors, astride a good horse, and around some of the finest folks who ever wore boots. Enjoy it.

GETTING STARTED

Fliers announcing team pennings are posted in tack, feed, and western-wear stores—and other places where horsemen will see them.

IF YOU have the penning bug, plus a horse, saddle, and trailer, you can probably find an arena within easy driving distance where you can begin. You really don't have to know anyone (penners are a friendly bunch and are enthusiastic about helping beginners), but you do have to find out where the action is.

Ask around among the horsemen that you know. One of them may have heard where pennings are being held. Check the bulletin boards at feed stores and tack shops. There may be notices posted of upcoming pennings. Look through your regional horse publications and the local newspaper classified section under "Live-stock" or "Horses for Sale." Arena opera-tors often run ads listing their schedules. Or, you can contact a local or regional team penning association and ask that the secretary send you a copy of the latest newsletter. It will list both sanctioned and practice pennings in your area.

Once you find out where the practice pennings are being held, you might wish to visit a time or two. That not only gives you the opportunity to familiarize your-self with the sport, but to introduce your-self to the penners as well. There's a good chance that you'll leave the arena with an invitation to "come pen with us soon."

Next, load Ol' Pet into the trailer and haul down for a practice session. Once you're there, saddle up and ride around. If you're not bashful, you can meet a lot of penners that way and probably be invited to join at least one team. Another way to get partnered is to tell the arena secretary that you are looking. He/she will probably announce it over the P.A. system and the

Penning action can be fast and furious, so don't be afraid to hang on to your saddle horn. Your team won't win anything if you lose your balance, throw the horse off stride, and let a cow get past you.

odds are that you'll find someone to ride with. Lots of team penners have started out just that way.

Once you get started penning, it's up to you as to how far you want to travel. You can stay close to home, competing in the practice/jackpot sessions and just have fun. Or, you can join one of the many team penning associations and go to the sanctioned events, competing for cash and year-end awards. At the top of the heap are the big, open events scattered across the county. That's where the real toughs are in action, but the amount of money that can be won there is well worth the effort.

Team penning is the fastest-growing western horse sport. It is fun, fast, and exciting; the competition adds spice to the event; and the people are great. But, be careful. Team penning can be habit-forming.

Many women are tough team penners, and all-ladies teams are not uncommon.

15

3 HORSES

Of major importance is a set of serviceable feet and legs that will stand up under continued hard use.

IF YOU'RE going to be a winner at team penning, you've got to be mounted. That means that the horse you're riding must be an asset, not a liability. There is no sense in making all that effort, and paying the entry fees, if the horse you are riding won't help. Like other contest mounts—cutting, reining, roping, 'dogging horses, working cow horses, and polo ponies—

team penning horses must meet certain basic requirements if they are going to do the job for you and stay sound. Conformation and bloodlines can vary, but all the good horses have many of the same characteristics.

Let's talk about some of the things to keep in mind when you're shopping for a team penning mount.

A ranch is a good place to look for a team penning prospect, as ranch horses usually handle well and have had lots of experience with cattle.

Photo by Gary Vorhes

16

Serviceable conformation and structural soundness. We all like to ride a good-looking horse, but lots of halter winners are not put together to really ride. Serviceable conformation means that the horse has a strong, functional bone structure with adequate muscling. He will have a good top line with a set of withers to hold the saddle in place, a sloping shoulder so that he has a good stride and can move, and not be so wide between the front legs that he can't turn around easily.

The hip should be fairly long, the loin strong, and the stifle stout 'cause that's where he's going to get the power to make those stops and turnarounds that it takes to help you win a penning. You also want the horse to be deep through the heart girth—"to cinch big"—so there's plenty of lung space and he can keep his speed up for 2 l-o-n-g minutes if he has to.

The neck should come out of the shoulder smoothly and not be too long or short since it helps the horse balance himself. The head . . . well, like a lot of cowboys, I figure that's just to hang the bridle on, but there has to be something in it. It's usually a pretty good idea to stay away from one of those Roman-nosed things. That bump seems to impair the horse's vision, and a horse needs to see as much as possible when he's trying to turn a cow.

Of major importance is a set of serviceable feet and legs that will stand up under continued hard use. The old adage, "No foot, no horse," holds true in team penning just as it does in any other performance event or on the racetrack. A horse is only as good as what he can do, and he must stay sound in order to do it. A team penning mount is a machine that can carry weight, is agile, and has enough speed to work cattle. In order for him to do that, all of his parts have to fit together and be strong enough to continue working.

Athletic ability. The horse must be able to handle himself, stop, and turn around quickly. That means he has to be a well-balanced athlete to perform all the moves that will be required in a penning. Some horses are, while others can't turn around in a 40-acre field. Riding some ol' puddin' foot at a penning is like tryin' to win a 100-yard dash wearing a pair of snowshoes. Watch your prospect move around some in the corral and then try him out. You can tell in a hurry if he is an athlete.

Handle. That just means that the pony

With his attention focused on the cow, this horse is showing the bred-in cow sense that a penning mount should have.

is well broke, and responsive to the reins. A horse that won't stop and turn around on command, no matter how fast he is moving, isn't going to get that yearling blocked and turned down the arena. All you have to do is ride a horse once to find out how well he can handle.

Cow sense. This is the inborn desire and ability that a horse has to "look at a cow" rather than just stampeding on by. Some horses have it and others don't— and you don't want the latter kind if you're going to team pen. Cow sense is the result of planned breeding programs and the majority of western horses have it, in varying degrees, in their backgrounds.

If you are looking at a prospect, it's safer to start with the raw material that has the potential ability, rather than an unknown. You don't raise race horses by crossing a plow horse with a Shetland pony, and the same is true with a cow horse. Some families of horses are known to be strong in cow sense and you might just as well capitalize on the fact. Cow sense is something that you can't see by just looking at a horse, but he'll sure give you the answer the first few times you ride him through a little bunch of cattle.

"Handle" means that the pony is well broke and responsive to the reins.

17

A cutting horse has a lot of cow sense and can make a good team penning mount. But first, he's got to learn to be aggressive toward cattle and drive them, rather than always staying back.

Right mental attitude. A good mental attitude is a necessity in a team penning mount. That means the horse is ready to work with you, can take the pressure of fast starts, stops, and turns time after time without blowing up or sulling when the action gets fast and furious. A horse can have all the other qualifications to be a top mount, but if his attitude isn't right and he can't take the pressure, you don't want him.

This isn't to say that a horse has to be a deadhead and put up with whatever happens. Many of the top performers are a little on the spooky side, have their little quirks, and have to be humored, but when the chips are down, you can sure win a penning on them.

There are enough good horses around that a penner doesn't have to put up with some broncy so-and-so that's cheating you every chance that he gets. There are too many of the good kind around to put up with the counterfeits.

Of course, some folks can get along

with a highly excitable individual while others need an easygoing pony that will put up with just about anything. Like people, horses are different, and matching a horse with a rider can sometimes take a lot of doing.

Background. Penning horses come from all types of backgrounds, conformation, and assorted bloodlines. They can be big, little, or in-between, although a big horse often isn't as quick on his feet as he needs to be. One of medium size (14.3 to 15.1 and 1,050 to 1,100 pounds) usually seems to fill the bill better than something larger. A small horse can be catty on his feet, but often doesn't have the weight-carrying ability, especially if a large man is on him. Of course, the only thing that really matters is whether he gets the job done and satisfies the rider.

One thing to remember: There is no such thing as the perfect horse. Choosing one is a compromise on how well the animal fits you and how capable he is in the arena. A horse can be a little short on cow

Rope horses usually won't make good penning mounts because they have been trained to run up on cattle, and then lock into place and rate them. They won't go by cattle to head and turn them back, which you must do in penning.

sense but make it up with handling and athletic ability. Or, he can lack agility but be long on try. The main factor: Does he fit you and can you win on him?

If you're buying a made horse, find one that suits you, meets the requirements, is sound mentally and physically, and is affordable. Don't take someone else's word that he is a penning horse. Go see him work and then try him out yourself—more than once. There are lots of good horses out there and there's bound to be one that will fit you. Just remember: You usually get about what you pay for, so don't expect to "steal" a good-looking, smooth-working horse that does it all on his own.

A horse that is only a prospect is something else, and that's where you need to keep the guidelines in mind.

I believe that you should look for a horse that is 4, 5, and up. He should be developed physically and mentally to stand up under use and pressure without blowing. A 2- or 3-year-old just doesn't

have the training or the physical and mental development to take the strain. In fact, a horse 6, 7, or 8 is in his prime and is just right as a penning prospect.

The best place to start looking for a penning prospect is on area ranches and feedlots, at cutting-horse and cow-horse training establishments, or from cowboys who do day work. These horses will have some age and experience on them, are usually pretty well broke, and have been exposed to cattle. They usually have serviceable conformation. They are also usually past the age where training accidents happen, which relieves you of another problem. Starting with a horse that has the basics and a lot of the bugs worked out makes the job a lot easier. Actually, with a horse like this, about all that you have to do is get him accustomed to the noise, excitement, and speed that is connected with team penning.

Cutting horses, and those that didn't quite make it as cutting horses, can be adapted to penning once they learn to

This is a good using horse, although not a halter horse. He has lots of bone, stands square, his knees and hocks are close to the ground, and he cinches deep. His back is fairly short, and he has a long underline, adequate hip, and a sloping shoulder. In other words, he's made to carry a rider and stay sound.

This head is not only pretty, but functional. The eyes are big, alert, and set to the side, and the nostrils are large. The head is also hung on the neck properly; i.e., the neck is longer at the poll than at the throatlatch. That means the horse can easily flex vertically— and can also breathe easily.

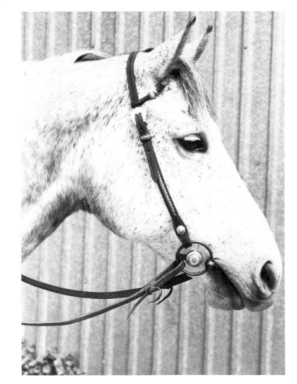

push and go by cattle instead of staying back. A turn-back horse is also another type that can rapidly make the switch to the penning arena. These horses have lots of "cow," and make penning lots of fun.

Some people pen on rope horses, but these ponies have been trained to run up behind a calf or steer and lock into place so the rider can make his throw. Sometimes it can be pretty hard to spur one on by, which you have to do in penning in order to head a steer and turn him back. On the other hand, these horses do have the advantage of being used to all the noise and confusion that is found around an arena.

A ranch or feedlot horse makes a great penning mount, as a general rule. This type has usually had about everything done on him that can be done around a cow. He will cut, block, or go past one to head it as needed, and is pretty level-headed. Theses horses have a broad-enough background and enough miles on

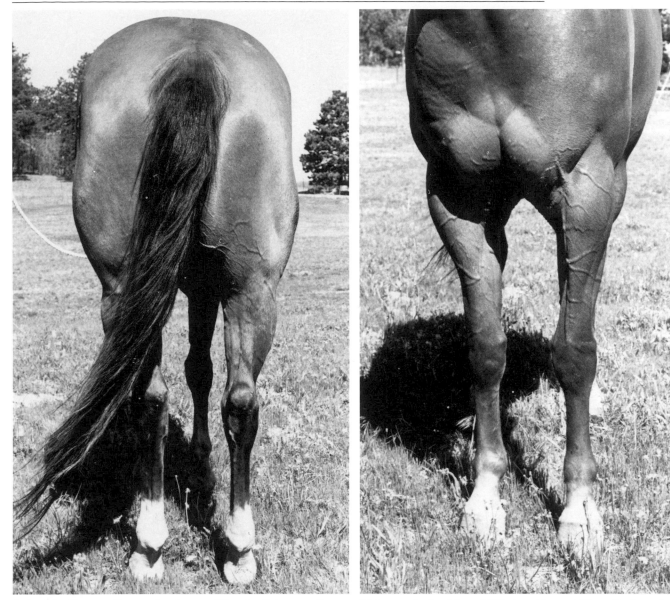

Lots of inside muscling and a strong stifle give this mare the power to make those quick stops and fast turns that team penning demands. She also stands squarely and well balanced, and has good bone.

This mare's chest is well V'ed and has width so the legs do not interfere with each other, but she's not so wide that she lacks agility. She also stands straight and square.

Some folks have been successful in taking a horse off the racetrack.

When you mash on the accelerator to get ahead of a cow to turn her back, your penning mount needs a quick burst of speed.

them that they don't get too excited about turning on the speed for a couple of minutes and then settling right back down.

Of course, a well-broke saddle horse with no prior ranch experience often makes the grade. If he has a rein (handle) on him and the right kind of mind, he can do the job. It usually doesn't take too much work to get this kind of horse looking at cattle, since many of the western breeds have some cow in their pedigree. If he has never been around cattle before, give him some time to get acquainted with the critters before jumping out and penning on him. That means riding around

and through a bunch of cattle, driving them in and out of the arena, and settling the herd. It usually doesn't take too long before Ol' Pet settles down and starts to pay attention.

Some folks have been successful in taking a horse off the racetrack, but that means a long retraining session before you can introduce him to cattle. A race horse has been trained to blow on past anything in front of him, and it will take a long, long time to get one slowed down and accept the rein. That rating back, or going by and then stopping and turning back, is something that is hard for a lot of horses to

The quick stops and turns made while working cattle put a lot of stress on a horse's bone and muscle structure. If he's not put together properly, he won't last long.

Buying a team penning mount is kinda like getting married.

do anyway, and it's doubly tough for a race horse to realize that he isn't going to just keep running.

Buying a team penning mount is kinda like getting married. Either the partnership works or it doesn't, and you'll find out soon enough. The main thing is to find a horse that meets most of your requirements and learn to get along with what doesn't fit. One thing for sure: You can't pen if you're not ahorseback. And, you've got to be mounted *right* to win.

4 CONDITIONING & KEEPING A HORSE FRESH

Diet is the first step.

TEAM PENNING is like any other speed event: Your horse needs to be in top physical condition to stand up to the strain and perform his best. That means a proper diet and a conditioning program to develop wind, tone muscles, build up energy, and sharpen the mind. Bringing a horse in from pasture and then expecting him to really work is not fair, and almost impossible. Of course, the same could be said for the rider, but we won't go into that.

At one time, athletes used to "play themselves into shape," but no more.

Coaches of all sports have realized that a regular conditioning program before the season starts will get their athletes into top shape faster and better. The same is true for your penning mount.

Diet is the first step. Get Ol' Pet in from pasture and then begin cutting down on the hay. At the same time, slowly increase the grain to provide necessary protein. While you are changing the ration to a "hotter" one, ride the horse each day, gradually increasing the time under saddle. Begin with lots of walking, some trotting,

Riding outside not only helps to condition your horse, but also gives him a change of pace from the hustle and excitement of team penning. It gives him a chance to relax, yet keeps him legged up.

and some loping to build up his wind, endurance, and muscle tone. His grass belly gradually disappears, his condition improves, he has more energy, and his responses to the bridle reins are quicker.

The horse's mind is becoming more alert and his body can respond. As the horse becomes more fit, you can increase the daily exercise. It usually takes a month to 6 weeks to get the horse in using shape so that his body can withstand the demands of penning.

This conditioning period is also a good time to go outside of the arena and ride across the pasture, trail ride, or just head up and down the road. Seeing new country and breaking the routine helps to keep the horse's mind fresh and responsive. If you have access to some cattle or a few goats, use them to sharpen up the pony's cutting skills, but don't get in a big hurry while you are doing it. Drive an animal around the arena and block it, cut one out, and let your horse work it a little, or just sit there, waiting for the cow to move so you can move with her. Before you know it, the horse will be reacting on his own.

When you start going to pennings, don't stop the outside riding. It's good for both of you. The open country and the change of scene not only helps keep the horse in shape, but can be a time of relaxation. You are not in a hurry, there aren't any cattle to push around, and you won't be jerking on the horse's head . . . and the horse will rapidly realize it. The change of

pace will pay off the next time you go to a penning. Your horse will be quieter, less excitable, and much easier to handle.

Like some barrel racing or rope horses, a penning mount can start anticipating a run as soon as he goes into the arena. He will start jumping around, try to head for the cattle before the signal is given, be difficult to control, and, in general, act silly. The best way to counteract this is to "score a bunch" at the practice sessions, just as ropers score their horses in the box to keep them from breaking too soon.

To score a penning horse, ride into the arena with another team and just sit there, well off to one side. When the team heads for the cattle, hold your horse back. If he gets agitated, circle him a couple of times, then walk out of the arena. Be sure that you're out of the arena before the team brings cattle up. Also, first ask the arena operator for permission to score your horse. It is a good exercise in control for your horse and teaches him to do what you want. It also makes him realize that he is not going to speed down the arena every time you ride in, and this helps to settle him down.

Settling the cattle between teams is another way to quiet a horse down, as well as getting him legged up. Loping

As the horse becomes more fit, you can increase the daily exercise.

25

Here's a mare in good condition for team penning or any other event.

This gelding is too fat. Until he's lost some weight, he won't have the wind or stamina for very many penning runs.

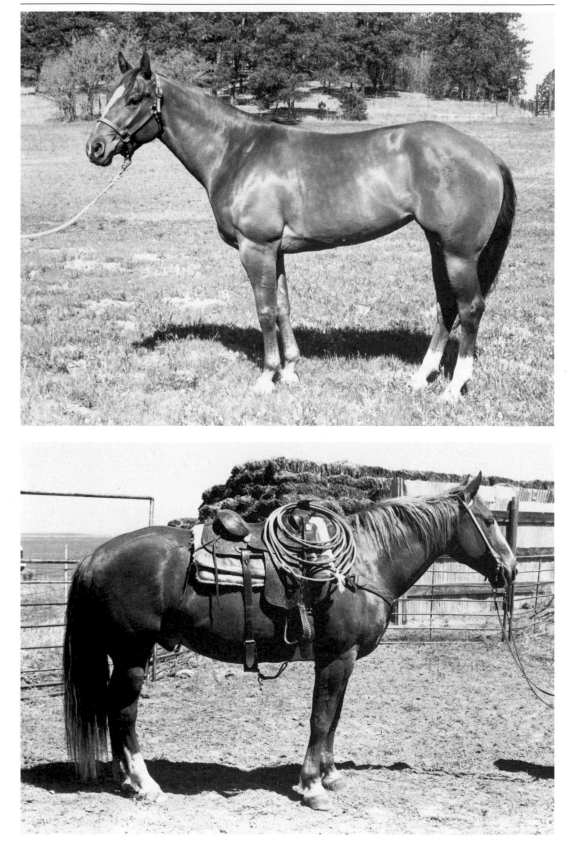

Riders warming up before a big team penning in Las Vegas.

down the arena, putting the cattle back into one bunch and holding them, then loping out of the arena time after time will do any penning mount lots of good. He learns that he isn't going to be chasing cattle every time he goes into the arena. Doing the same thing time after time eventually relaxes him so he takes things easy.

Warming Up

Get to the penning in plenty of time to warm your horse up before you work. If his muscles aren't ready for it, a sudden burst of action can sometimes cause him to injure himself. You want to give your horse every opportunity to perform at his best, and he can't do that if he's "cold."

Start out walking until he seems to be moving easily. Then speed up to a long trot. After you have trotted in circles until his head is down and the edge off him, move on to a lope. Make sure that the horse lopes in the proper lead at all times. You want to get the muscles loosened up, plus get your horse collected and his mind responsive.

Just before you pen, you might lope out a ways, stop, and then spin around a time or two, just to remind him that he'll need to do that later on. If possible, volunteer to settle the cattle. (You can't do this with the cattle in the section that you and your team will be working.) Loping in and out of the arena will not only help warm your horse up, but take some of the edge off as well. During this warm-up period, you don't need to really pull your cinches tight, but you do want them snug enough that the saddle won't turn. Just before you work, step off, reset your saddle, and then pull the cinches tight.

Take advantage of the time before your run to get your horse ready, both physically and mentally. It increases your chances for a good performance.

Scoring a penning horse helps him to settle down because he soon learns he's not going to gallop down the arena every time you ride in. To score, ride into the arena with another team, and hold your horse back when the other team heads for the cattle. After a few times, your horse will be much quieter.

Here's a good example of a horse that's too excited and won't stand still behind the starting line. He could get his rider hurt with his rearing and acting up.

Riding one and leading another to warm up before a penning contest starts.

Horse Sense

There are several things to keep in mind around a penning. Always be aware of where your horse is tied and what he is tied to. A lot of time is spent just waiting, and for a horse, that means being tied. Before you leave home, make sure that's one lesson the animal has learned thoroughly, even if it means enforcing things with a set of hobbles for a while. Standing tied is one of the basics that every horse should know, but a lot of them don't.

Try not to tie up too close to other horses, especially an individual with a yellow ribbon tied in his tail (that means he kicks) or some cranky ol' mare. The first thing you know, your horse is kicked and you might be out of competition for a while. Be sure that what you tie to is solid enough that it will hold the horse, not something that he can pull loose, stampede with, and injure himself. And, those bridle reins are meant to guide with, not to tie with. A halter and rope is a lot stouter. Broken bridle reins or a torn-up headstall

means a loose horse and that can easily translate into more loose horses and possible injury.

Make sure that the cinches are pulled tight before you ride into the arena. Some folks forget, and having a saddle turn can be, at the very least, embarrassing. Horses, even the best of them, can come untrained when the saddle and the rider begin slipping off to one side. After you've made your run, loosen the cinches instead of just tying the horse and walking off. All of us have seen a horse tied up, pawin' a hole in the ground, and restless because he's uncomfortable from a tight girth.

Since the majority of pennings last most of the day, you'll need to water your horse before the day is over. Take your own bucket along and teach him to drink out of that. There is usually a handy water spigot or hydrant, and your own bucket is safer than using one of those community

Always be aware of where your horse is tied and what he is tied to.

29

Team penning horses spend lots of time tied to a fence or trailer. Make sure you always tie to something stout, and away from other horses that might kick. Also, tying with a halter and lead rope prevents a lot of broken reins, and your horse will be there when you come back.

Get your horse accustomed to drinking out of a bucket before going to pennings or other horse events.

Some horses will ground-tie, especially ranch horses. But it's usually not a good idea to ground-tie at a penning (or other event) because the horse could wander off and get into trouble—like getting kicked by tied-up horses.

troughs. Your horse could pick up a disease or illness drinking out of one.

Strange as it seems, some horses don't know how to, or won't, drink out of a bucket. This is sometimes true of horses that have always watered out of a stream or big stock tank. Train such a horse at home by only offering him water in a bucket for several days, or add some sweet syrup, like Karo, to the water. If your horse is finicky about drinking strange water away from home, add a flavoring to his water that makes all water smell and taste the same.

One last thing. When you're going down the road, it's a good idea to have a simple equine first-aid kit along. Things can happen and you need to be prepared. You'll need some kind of antiseptic salve, leg wraps and bandages, maybe some Bute for minor lameness or soreness, something for minor colic (ask your vet what he recommends), and maybe a couple of doses of tranquilizer. A twitch is also handy to have. Hopefully, you'll never need any of this, but it's best to be prepared just in case.

5   EQUIPMENT

Team penners ride one of two styles of seats.

LIKE MANY things in the horse world, saddle styles are constantly changing, and it's up to you to decide if you want to add another saddle to your collection when you take up team penning. But as long as the saddle that you are currently riding has a strong tree, stout rigging, fits both you and your horse, and satisfies you, I don't believe that you need another one.

The majority of saddles made today are double rigged; that is, have both a front cinch and back cinch. The rigging can be the traditional ring-on-the-tree variety, or a steel plate in the skirt. Both are stout and will pull down snugly on a horse. One advantage of a double rig: It makes the saddle sit down tighter on a horse's back when he makes fast stops and turns.

If you do ride with a back cinch, make sure it's snugged up against the belly so the horse can't put a back foot through it, and so it doesn't hang up on something. People who ride with too much slack in their back cinches might as well take them off. Not only are they useless that way, they are dangerous.

Team penners ride one of two styles of seats. One is the conventional seat that has a slight rise in front, and the other is the flat-seat cutter. The latter is usually an inch or two longer than the seat in a conventional saddle. Why? A cutting horse rider "floats" with the horse, instead of sitting deep, and needs the extra length. Use whichever seat you feel the most secure in.

Stirrups

The Visalia, bell-bottom, and roper styles all have a flat bottom that is easy on the foot, especially for folks who wear flat-arch roper boots. Stirrups come in tread widths from 1 to 4 inches, with the 2½- and 3-inch being the most common. You can get any of these styles in wood, both plain and metal-bound, leather or rawhide covered, or in cast iron and aluminum.

Oxbows were originally designed by bronc riders, since they are easier to hold on a real active horse, and for years the only place you saw them was on contest bronc saddles. Now, cutters, barrel racers, and a number of ranch cowboys are using them. The bottoms are rounded, to fit the arch of a boot, and the tread width is usu-

Here's a good-looking horse with good equipment at a Las Vegas penning. This rider is using reins and a romal, which are popular in the far West.

This saddle has a full-double, on-the-tree rigging with steel dees, and fits the horse properly. If the bars of a tree are too wide, the saddle sits too low and can pinch the withers. If they are too narrow, the saddle sits too high, and tends to roll. A rule of thumb: A saddle fits properly if you can slide your flat hand between the gullet and the blanket.

This is another photograph of the same saddle, showing a better view of the seat, which is typical of the seat in most western saddles.

ally 1 inch (except the contest version which is narrower). Oxbows can be made of wood, shaped steel, cast iron, or aluminum, and may or may not be covered with leather or rawhide.

Saddle Pads and Blankets

Probably the most comfortable and economical pad available today is the synthetic fleece pad. It can have fleece on both sides, or a blanket top, and can have ³/₄- or 1-inch felt slipped between the fleece and the top. These pads are soft and absorbent, conform to a horse's back, and can be easily cleaned by hosing the sweat out of them. They come in various thicknesses, and some have enough cushioning so another blanket is not necessary. When new, they are a little slippery, but once they are broken in, they work fine.

A lot of folks combine one of the thinner fleece pads with a Navajo-type blanket on top. That's enough cushioning for most riding jobs, and the Navajo-type blanket adds a lot of color. Of course, you can use a real Navajo, but it's so durn expensive you hate to put it next to the horse and sweat it out.

When buying a pad or blanket, get one with wear leathers on each side. They don't add much to the cost and will prolong the life of the pad or blanket considerably. Latigos and billet straps will wear right through any kind of cloth in just a few months if it is not protected.

Some riders figure that if one pad is good, two are better, and they stack a couple of thick ones on a horse and then add the saddle. With a horse that has an average back, the saddle sits too high above the withers. That makes the seat run downhill so you can't ride correctly and, no matter how tight you pull the

When the back end of the saddle raises up like this during quick stops and turns, it can throw the rider off balance, and will thump the horse's back. You can prevent this from happening by using a back cinch, and snugging it up against the belly. This saddle does have a back cinch, but evidently it is too loose.

A flat-seat cutter with full-double, on-the-tree rigging, cushioned seat, and the oxbow stirrups that are preferred by many cutters and team penners. The flat seat allows the rider to "float" during the action, rather than sitting deep, as in a conventional seat.

latigos, the saddle still rolls like you're riding it on a barrel. Protect your horse's back, but don't use so much that the saddle won't stay in place.

Breast Collars

Some riders use 'em, some don't. As a general rule, however, a properly adjusted breast collar will help keep your saddle from slipping back on a hard-turning, hard-starting penning horse. Even if the saddle fits the horse, the padding is correct, and the horse's back is conformed to carry a saddle, the fast action can move things around. A breast collar helps keep the saddle in place.

The most popular and effective breast collar style for penners is the type that attaches to both rigging rings (or small D rings in the front of the skirts). It also has a hold-down strap that runs between the front legs to the center of the cinch. The three-point hookup not only keeps the saddle in place, but holds the collar down so it won't choke the horse.

Bridles

These come in so many styles and materials that all anyone can say is to use what you like and what you've got. There are browband, shaped-ear, split-ear, slot-ear, and no-ear headstalls, and they can be made from leather, braided rawhide, nylon, braided nylon cord, and even braided binder twine, so . . . take your choice. Just be sure that whatever you use is in good

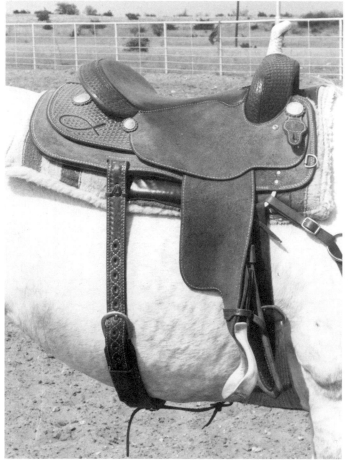

Another flat-seat cutter, but with in-skirt rigging, which drops the front rigging down lower. This allows the saddle to pull down well on the horse, and also allows the stirrup leathers to swing forward more easily. And it puts less bulk under the rider's knees. This photo also shows how the back cinch should be pulled up snug against the belly.

Here's a well-worn saddle that has seen lots of miles in the Texas brush country. The seat rises slightly in the front, making it a little narrower and more comfortable to ride for long periods. The saddle has full-double, on-the-tree rigging, and rawhide-covered bell-bottom stirrups with a 3-inch tread.

repair and securely fastened to the bit. Having a headstall break during a penning run can be plumb exciting . . . for both you and the crowd.

Bridle Reins

Reins are another personal preference, but the majority of penners seem to favor split reins over the one-piece roper rein. Using split reins, a rider can adjust his slack by sliding and pulling the reins through his fingers. He also has a lot more rein in the first place, making it easier to stay off the horse's mouth.

The length of a roping rein is fixed. This is a disadvantage in penning because when the action gets fast, it's too easy to raise your rein hand too high, which automatically brings up the horse's head. With split reins, you can feed enough slack so your

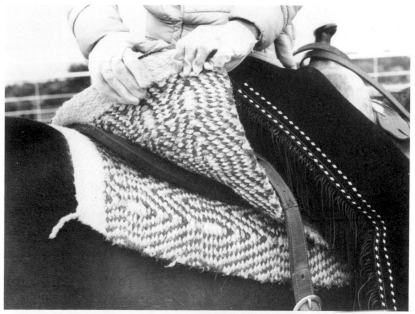

This is a double-woven saddle blanket with a felt pad slipped between the folds for a little more cushioning.

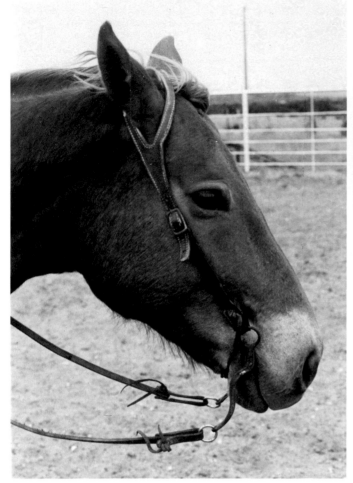

A one-ear headstall with curb bit, and reins securely attached with leather string.

This is a sliding-ear headstall with curb bit. Note how the reins attach to the bit with latigo leather string—which is safer than snaps. A cavesson has also been fashioned out of leather string to keep the horse's mouth shut.

horse can get his head down to see the cattle and work.

Harness, bridle, strap, and latigo leathers are the materials most commonly used for reins (lots of penners are using the long, heavy, harness-leather cutting horse reins), but nylon, braided nylon cord, or soft rope are popular with some riders. The big thing: Make sure the reins are securely attached to the bit with something that won't break or work loose at the wrong time. Leather tie thongs work better than Chicago screws or snaps, both of which can come undone.

Bits

There have been numerous books written on this subject and they all end up saying the same thing: Use what works best on your horse for the job that you are doing. Not all horses will work equally well with the same bit, so experiment until

you find one that your mount accepts. Of course, there are some horses that will work with anything, and others for whom nothing seems to fit; but, generally, there is a bit for every horse.

Go to enough team pennings, cuttings, ropings, barrel races, and playdays, and you'll see just about every kind of bit made—plus some homemade contraptions that defy description.

The ring snaffle is the basic bit and from there, it is all uphill. The trick is to find the least amount of cheek/mouthpiece that your horse will pay attention to and use that. Long shanks on a curb bit are supposed to add "whoa," but a long-shank bit can also pull a horse's head around and unbalance him if you take ahold while you're trying to head a cow.

It's been said a lot of times before, but a bit to a horse is like a boot to you. It's possible to walk in a number of different styles of boots, but some are a lot more

A snaffle bit and running martingale make one of the best combinations for team penning. The snaffle allows direct reining, which is often more effective than neck reining when the action gets fast and furious; and the running martingale helps keep the head in position.

Here's a noseband made from doubled and stitched latigo leather. Note how the tie-down strap runs through a small leather loop tied to the breast collar. This is a safety factor. When the horse drops his head to graze or drink, he could put a foot over the tie-down strap if it's not held up by such a loop.

comfortable. The same goes for your horse and bits.

Tie-downs

Team penning is judged on time. Because the action gets fast and furious, frequently the rider's rein hand gets too high. When that happens, the horse's head also goes up and he can't see where he's going. Also, he can't stop and turn around like he can when his head is down near shoulder height, and he loses the ability to handle cattle quickly. A tie-down limits just how high his head can go. This improves the rider's control and the horse's line of vision.

Using a tie-down is NOT poor horse-manship, as some people believe. It is taking advantage of a tool that has been around for centuries to help control your mount at speed. Ropers and barrel racers learned long ago that keeping the horse's head down, out of their way and so he could see where he was going, improved their chances of winning. And, winning is the name of the game.

If your horse will work without one, great. But if he won't, and there are many horses that won't keep their heads down when they get excited, or if you can't keep your hands down, use one.

There are a number of tie-down styles, and it's up to you to decide what will work best in your particular case. Just be sure that if you haven't used one before, you let the horse get used to it in the corral first. Adjust it correctly and turn the horse loose. Horses have been known to flip over backwards the first time they felt their heads restrained, and you don't want to be aboard if that happens. The adjustment—how far you bring the head down—depends on the individual horse. Some need more slack than others.

This is a combination bonnet/noseband tie-down made from vinyl-covered steel cable. It applies pressure on both the poll and nose.

Nosebands for tie-downs can be made of lariat rope, braided rawhide, braided nylon cord, flat leather or nylon, steel cable or rod, and even chain. If the tie-down strap is too tight, nosebands made of cable, rod, rope, or chain will cut a horse's nose.

One other note: A tie-down that attaches to a noseband also prevents the horse from pushing his nose out to get away from the bit.

Bonnet. This is one type of tie-down that has a double-loop arrangement of rope, cable, or chain that goes over the horse's forehead and over the poll (behind the ears), and is then attached to the cinch by an adjustable strap. A bonnet will hold the horse's head down, but does not limit how far he can push his nose out to get away from the bit.

Combination noseband/bonnet. This double-duty tool applies pressure to both the top of the head and the nose, and takes hold of a horse rather severely. The

majority of bonnets are made from vinyl-covered cable that attaches to the cinch with an adjustable strap.

Most horsemen who use a tie-down attach a small loop (about 6 inches deep) to the front of the breast collar and run the adjustment strap from the noseband to the cinch through it. This prevents the strap from dropping when the horse lowers his head to graze or drink—resulting in his possibly getting a front foot caught in it.

Running martingale. This is not a tie-down, but limits the height of the rider's pull on the horse's head. The rings are usually set at wither height, keeping the pull low so that the animal does not raise his head. A running martingale is best used with a ring snaffle, not a shanked bit.

Protective Boots

It's wise to use splint boots and bell boots (overreach boots). A horse can overreach and nick a front foot or cannon bone, and you're afoot until he heals up. A horse won't work properly if he's hurt, or afraid of hurting himself, so why take chances?

Splint boots (around the cannon bones) and bell boots are well worth their cost. They can prevent the horse from injuring himself if he strikes a front foot against the opposite leg, or overreaches, during penning action.

6 THE ARENA

An arena too large wears out the cattle.

SINCE ARENA sizes and shapes vary across the country, there are no official plans or dimensions that must be followed. Penners ordinarily adapt an existing rodeo, horse show, or roping arena to their needs. An excessively large arena (one more than 250-300 feet long) is so big that the cattle wear out quickly from running up and down. Often, the large arenas are shortened for penning by running a fence of steel panels across them.

The arena format shown in this chapter seems to be the most effective. It allows the cattle ample opportunity to test a team's ability, yet is small enough to give the riders some control of the cattle. The proportions shown give riders a maximum working area to cut out cattle without excessive fouling problems. Normally, 60 percent of the arena from the back end, where the cattle are held, to the start/foul line is the free zone. An additional 15 percent, making a total of 75 percent of the arena, is added from the start/foul line to

This is the arena at Horseman's Park, a county-owned facility in Las Vegas. The arena measures 326 by 168 feet, and is used for team pennings, rodeos, and other events. Those three riders in the background are herd holders hightailing it out of the arena (through a side gate) as a team starts its run.

40

Most pens are built from steel or pipe panels, which are sturdy and easy to set up. This photo also shows the judge positioned at the pen, ready to drop his flag when (if) the team gets its three head penned.

Here's the line judge at Horseman's Park. He is stationed on the start/foul line, which is an imaginary line between his position and a flag opposite him on the No. 4 chute.

the front of the pen.

In an extremely short arena, the pen might have to be moved farther away from the herd end of the arena to leave adequate working room. Then the distance from the pen gate to the back of the arena will be less than the suggested 75 percent. Occasionally an arena will be so short that the back of the pen will have to be set on the start/foul line.

Recommended Arena Dimensions

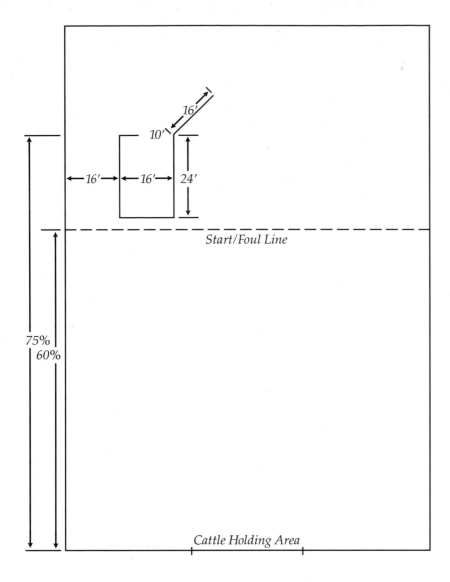

Start/Foul Line

75%
60%

Cattle Holding Area

The start/foul line should be well marked so both the riders and the line judge can see it. The best way is to either attach a flag to the arena fence at that point on either side, or to wrap colored ribbon around the posts. Orange or red is more easily noticed than other colors.

Some arena operators "fill in the corners" by setting a fence panel across a square corner at a 45-degree angle. This prevents cattle from bunching up or locking, and allows the penners to keep the cattle moving with no hangups. These panels must be well secured since they might take a lot of hits as the yearlings crash into them.

The arena fence must be stout enough, and high enough, to hold the cattle once they are stirred up during the penning. More than one yearling has managed to get over a 5-foot fence. Don't ever sell 'em short. A milling bunch of yearlings can also do a pretty good job of tearing up a fence, and a herd of wild ones can finish the job. Whether it's welded pipe, crossties and wire, or what-have-you, it has to be stout. That's an advantage of most rodeo arenas, and why they make ideal penning locations.

Pen. Dimensions are 16 by 24 feet deep with a 10-foot-wide gate and a 16-foot wing. Originally, the pen was 16 by 16 feet, but it was soon learned that more depth allowed the cattle to slow down before they hit the back end. That not only eliminated some roughing calls against riders who jammed their cattle clean to the back, but also kept the arena crew from making so many trips into the arena to straighten the pen up.

Most pens are made from steel or pipe fence panels joined together. At each corner, steel fence posts are driven into the ground *inside* the pen. This provides

This photo shows the herd end of the Windy Ryon Arena at Saginaw, Texas. This arena is 330 feet long and 250 feet wide at the herd end. That width not only tires horses and cattle, but requires a change in strategy by team penners. In order to make fast times, they can't use the side fences to help sort out their three head.

a solid anchor for tying the panels. Don't, however, set a post at either the end of the gate or the end of the wing. That can cost a rider his knee if he hits it hard enough. The wing is set at a 45-degree angle from the end of the gate.

The entire pen is set parallel to the side of the arena with a 16-foot alley, or "hole." Some penning contests insist on more room here, but it makes the chore of keeping the cattle from stampeding past the hole rider almost impossible. There is just too much ground to cover.

Ground. Keep the ground worked up and loose so that the horses and cattle can handle it. If the footing is too hard and slick, a horse or cow can slip and go down. Wetting the arena down before a penning to control dust is always appreciated, but don't get it too wet, causing it to be slippery. Team penning can be dusty and dirty, for both contestants and spectators, so make things as comfortable as possible, but not dangerous. Also, if there is too much dust, the penners can't read the numbers on the cattle.

7 BREEDS & TYPES OF CATTLE

Team penners should be familiar with the characteristics of the different breeds and types.

THE MOST popular penning cattle are 400- to 550-pound crossbred heifers. These cattle are light enough to be active, have usually not been handled so much that they have lost respect for a horse, and—unless they get too tired—can stand up under penning action. However, penners usually cannot choose the cattle they'd like for a contest, so they should be familiar with the different breeds and types of cattle, and understand some of their characteristics.

Cattle come in assorted breeds and combinations of breeds—with varying temperaments and degrees of wildness, or ease of handling. In addition, previous handling—and the skill of the people who did the handling—all have an effect on cattle.

The head is the most reliable indicator of a cow's temperament. *Generally*, cattle with large, soft eyes set well on the sides of the head, with a broad forehead, are quieter, less flighty, and easier to work than are narrow-headed cows with small, beady eyes set close together. The placement of the eyes affects how a cow sees and, as a result, how she will handle. This is covered in detail in the next chapter.

Here's a nice set of yearlings, settled in the middle of the arena and awaiting the first team of penners.

Incidentally, although a herd of cattle might contain steers, heifers, and/or cows, we will just use the term cow throughout this book.

Usually, a herd of cattle provided for a penning will be fairly uniform, containing cattle of the same basic breeding, age, and weight. But sometimes the herd will have different types of cattle, and a penner must adjust his strategy as necessary. Watching the cattle while they are being worked will tell a penner a lot regarding how they should be handled.

There are four basic types of cattle that might be provided for a penning contest. They are: British beef breeds and crossbreds, dairy cattle, crossbred Brahmas, and Longhorns and Corrientes. Each type has its own peculiarities and temperament and must be handled accordingly.

British breeds. These cattle—both the purebreds and crossbreds—are the most popular for penning and with commercial cattlemen. They include Herefords, with the familiar red bodies and white trim; Angus, that are solid black; and Shorthorns, whose colors include pure white, deep red, and a lot of red roans. These breeds are termed British since they all originated in the British Isles.

Several other European breeds have become popular in the United States in recent years, and among them are the Charolais, Chianina (pronounced KEY-a-nee-na), and Simmental.

The crossbreds of all the above breeds are blocky, have some leg under them, have squared, alert heads, wide-set eyes, medium-size ears, and come in a variety of colors. They are *usually* fairly gentle and will respect a horse. But if they are range cattle and have only seen an occasional man or horse, they might bulldoze anything in their path.

As a general rule, these crossbreds settle well, stay bunched as a herd, and can be cut out by a rider. On the downside, hot, humid weather can be hard on them because of their heavier coats, and they can't take as much use as the Brahma crossbreds, Longhorns, or Corrientes.

Dairy cattle. Because these cattle have had continuous contact with man, they are usually gentler and more tractable than the beef breeds. Good-natured and easy to handle, they are not prone to getting excited—although all cattle are unpredictable and anything can happen. As a general

Some of those ol' long-headed Brahmers don't pay much attention to a horse.

rule, the dairy breeds and crossbreds will not be as quick as some of the other types, nor will they have the endurance. Therefore they will tire more easily, and when they do, they will sull up and won't drive.

When dairy cattle are used for a penning contest, they are usually the familiar black-and-white Holsteins, but sometimes Guernseys and Jerseys are used.

Brahmas. Few purebred Brahmas are used for penning contests as they can be too flighty and difficult to handle. But "Brahmers" have been crossed with many breeds, and the resulting crossbreds are popular with many cattlemen. Just a few include Brangus (Brahma/Angus), Charbray (Charolais/Brahma), and Braford (Brahma/Hereford).

Depending on the amount of Brahma blood these crossbred cattle carry (it can

45

Herefords have red bodies and white trim.

The term "ear cattle" refers to those cattle that have the long, droopy ears indicative of Brahma breeding.

range from 1/8th to 7/8ths), they can still show some characteristics of the European breeds; but the big ears, slightly domed profile, and nervous disposition reveal their Brahma ancestry. As a side note, their big ears have given rise to the term "ear cattle." When you hear this term used, it means the cattle have some Brahma blood.

In color, Brahma crossbreds range from almost pure white (or cream) to black, with other solid colors, paints, and tiger-stripe brindles in between. These cattle are smart, alert, aggressive, and very active.

The most effective way to handle Brahma crossbreds is to give them plenty of room, and not get them hot and angry. If a rider crowds them too much, they have been known to jump the nearest fence or run over the rider. If they decide to go back to the herd, or down the alley (between the pen and fence), they can be nearly impossible to stop.

When they come into the arena, these Brahma crossbreds will have their heads up, looking around at the strange surroundings. Normally, they will respect a horse and can be turned—and can be successfully penned, sometimes in very rapid times. But they *can* run, are often eager to do so, and can make things exciting.

When the announcer calls your number and the cattle carrying it are long-headed, narrow-faced "Brahmers" that have their heads up and are looking for a hole so they can escape, get set to ride!

Corrientes and Longhorns. These two are grouped together because of their horns, varied coloring, and the fact that they handle very much alike. Corri-

One black yearling (arrow) in a herd of Hereford cattle gives an unfair advantage to the team drawing the number worn by the black. Most contractors who supply cattle for pennings try to keep the cattle within a herd all one color, or a good mixture of colors.

ente cattle are usually imported out of old Mexico for roping and bulldogging—although there are some Corriente breeders in the United States now. These cattle are tough, quick, and alert—and the older ones have a pretty good horn spread, which means don't crowd them or your horse might get hooked.

If Corrientes have *not* been used for roping, they are a challenge to team penners and can stand lots of use. But once they have been roped, they lose respect for horses and will not handle easily. For example, you can't easily drive them; they just won't move willingly. While they can be penned, don't expect anything sensational because you really have to push them around. And generally, once a roping steer decides he's going thataway, he *will* go thataway, despite your efforts to stop him. Respecting a

A black baldy is usually a crossbred Hereford/ Angus.

horse isn't really a part of his makeup. The only way that you will turn one of these freight trains is with a rope, and that's not a part of team penning.

Longhorns are usually faster than Corrientes, speedier than a lot of horses, and are

47

There's a good mix of colors in this nice set of cattle.

also smart, agile, and very alert. Normally they will respect a horse. But if they have been roped a lot before being used for team penning, sometimes they don't pay much attention to riders. For most riders, working Longhorns means that the team will have to "cowboy up," since these cattle can be a little difficult to handle, primarily due to their speed.

Summary. In a sanctioned team penning contest, cattle are grouped 30 to a herd. The cattle within a herd should be uniform in size—and either all of one color, or a good mixture of colors. Although it can be difficult for a team to spot their cattle in a herd of all Herefords, or all Angus, at least all the teams working that herd have the same problem.

Another factor that should be mentioned is the luck of the draw. Regardless of how well you handle cattle, no matter how many contests you and your partners have won, or how good your horses are, Lady Luck will play a big role in whether you go to the pay window. You can draw good cattle, or you can draw bad cattle. And cattle, being what they are, don't always do what they are supposed, or expected, to do. In fact, if they follow the rules about 65 percent of the time, you can count yourself lucky.

There are going to be contests where Lady Luck rides along on your shoulder. The cattle assigned to you are standing in a tight group on the edge of the herd and almost outrun your horses speeding up the arena and into the pen, and all three remain in the pen until the flag drops.

Other days, nothing will go right. Your cattle hide in the herd, double back after they've been cut out, duck past the horse in the alley, or an extra steer goes into the pen with your three and won't leave his buddies. Or there will be times when the entire herd scatters up the arena like a covey of quail when your cutter rides in. If the turn-back riders can't hold them, they will stampede across the foul line and you'll be disqualified.

Be prepared for both kinds of luck . . . that's team penning.

A typical Corriente.

8 HOW CATTLE SEE & REACT

A team penner must know when to push cattle, and when to back off and give them room.

TO BE successful at team penning, a contestant must develop an understanding of cattle. Handling cattle well requires that a penner be able to take advantage of their nature and characteristics.

A team must be loaded with cow sense, quick reflexes, and a liberal dose of luck to cut three head out of the herd and haze them down the arena and into the pen in winning time. A penner must be aware of how a cow will probably react to a rider in various situations, and he must know where to position himself to obtain the

desired result. He must also understand that different breeds and types of cattle must be handled according to their individual temperaments and dispositions. And perhaps most important, he must know when to push cattle, and when to back off and give them room.

The top penners are instinctively aware of all these factors every time they ride into the arena. They don't have to think about what to do; they simply react. Consequently, they respond instantly to the changing conditions and actions of the

Top team penners are instinctively aware of how cattle react to riders in various situations and positions.

50

cattle, and use their knowledge of bovine nature to control them. In fact, some of these penners are such good cow psychologists they can look at a set of yearlings and almost predict how every individual in the herd will work. That's what's known as being able to read cattle.

Like horses, sheep, goats, and deer, cattle are "flight animals" in the wild; running is their principal defense from predators. Flight is also their automatic response to a threat, and to cattle, a rider is a threat.

For defensive purposes, a cow has a wide angle of vision so she can see danger soon enough to take flight. Therefore, nature has positioned the cow's eyes on the sides of the head, rather than in front as with predators such as dogs and cats, and man. This increased peripheral vision (figure A) improves the cow's chances of staying alive in the wild.

A cow cannot see directly behind her body because of her eye position and her body's bulk. But, she can raise and turn her head, looking back over her hip, to see what is behind her and to one side. She still has the blind zone, but it's in a different position (figures B and B-1).

The cow also has a blind zone for 10 to 15 feet directly in front of her, because of the way her eyes are positioned. Each eye sees individually, and the two vision paths do not come together until they reach a point 10 to 15 feet in front of the cow (figure A). This is why cattle will sometimes crash into a fence, or any other object directly in front of them; they do not see the object in time to stop.

The cow's peripheral vision, and how she reacts to what she sees and doesn't see, provides the major key in how to handle her. When you are off to one side of her, she can see you, and you can make her turn away from you. Even if you are 50 feet out to one side, she can still see you, and you can stop or turn her without getting much closer.

When you are directly behind the cow, however, she can't see you. She just knows you are there, and runs even faster to try and escape. This is okay IF she is headed in the direction you want her to go. But if you want to turn her, you've got to move parallel to her, into her vision zone. But do not move right alongside her.

Not only can the cow see you better when you are some distance away from her, it's safer. If you are too close to her,

A cow's eyes are set on the side to give her a wide angle of vision.

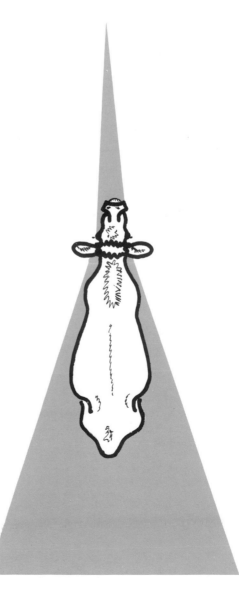

Figure A. Because of where the cow's eyes are positioned, she cannot see directly in front of her for 10 to 15 feet, or directly behind her. The gray areas indicate her blind zones.

51

Figure B. When the cow raises and turns her head, she can see what's behind her, on one side.

Figure B-1. Her blind zone shifts to the other side when she turns her head the other way.

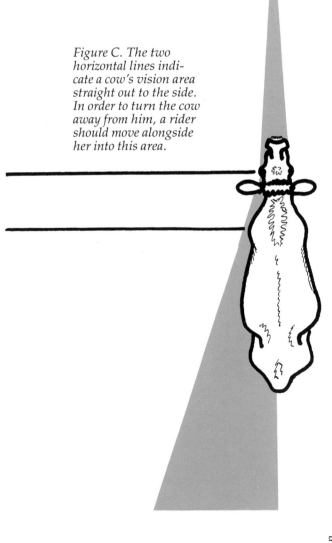

Figure C. The two horizontal lines indicate a cow's vision area straight out to the side. In order to turn the cow away from him, a rider should move alongside her into this area.

and she decides to turn into your path, she will probably collide with your horse and cause a wreck.

Another reason to keep some distance between you and the cow: It gives you some room to maneuver if she suddenly stops, or turns away from you. If you are right next to her, you have no room to stop and turn to stay with her. Then you must play catch-up.

This happens all the time in the fence work in cow-horse classes. The horse is so close to the cow when he goes by to block her and turn her back on the fence that after she turns, she can escape to the middle of the arena. Although the block and turn might look flashy, the horse has actually lost control of the cow.

To maintain control, you need to be out and away from the cow. Then when she stops or turns, you have room to also stop and turn—and stay right with her.

A cow must also be *aware* of a rider in order to be controlled. Shouting, popping a hand on your chaps, waving your free arm, or swinging your bridle reins all help to get her attention, and keep it on you. A cow will signal when she is paying attention to you, even if she is moving and is some distance away. She will turn her head slightly toward you to bring you into her vision area, and she will slightly drop the ear on that side.

Another bovine trait that penners should be aware of is her instinct. Cattle prefer to stay within the bunch, evidently

This rider has moved up almost opposite the cow's shoulder and is staying out where she can see him. He's also yelling at her, to help make her turn and go up the arena toward the pen.

This rider was trying to send the light-colored yearling back to the herd, by blocking her on the fence and turning her back. But after going by the cow, she couldn't get stopped, and lost control of the cow.

53

It looks like this rider is trying to turn the cow back the other way—toward the pen. If so, he's not going to get the job done because he's much too close to her. She's going to highball it right on down the fence and back to the herd.

The herd instinct makes handling two cows easier than handling one. It also makes it more difficult to separate a pair of buddies when they don't have matching numbers. Notice how the rider is staying out to the side where the cows can see her. As a result, they should turn up the arena, toward the pen.

One cow out and the second one headed towards her. The first cow is usually the hardest one to cut and move down the arena. But once she's out, it's easier to head the second and third cows up the arena in her direction because of the herd instinct.

feeling that there is safety in numbers. Therefore, they can sometimes be hard to separate. They will, however, move to another animal, or animals, much easier than they will trot down the arena to a wide expanse of nothing.

Often, the hardest animal of the three to cut out is the first one. Once she is out and standing where she can be seen, the second and third cows will usually join her when the cutter applies the pressure to push them out of the herd. Of course, when two cows have buddied up but their numbers are not the same, splitting the pair can be tough. Or, maybe the one that should go back to the herd decides to drift up and stay with his/her friend, adding trash that the penners must contend with.

This herd instinct can be used to a penner's advantage if he will, when the opportunity offers, keep two animals together in either cutting or driving. They draw confidence from each other and will handle easier as a pair than they will singly. This trait is of major importance at the pen end of the arena. Get the three head together as quickly as possible before trying to pen them. If one breaks off, try to regroup them, because they'll head through that gate a lot better as a bunch.

Driving Cattle

Push cattle from behind and off to the left or right. Remember a cow's vision area, and stay where she can see you, on the side away from the direction that you will later turn her. Make sure that you keep her attention focused on you by yelling or waving an arm. If you are pushing her up the arena, away from the herd, make sure you can block her if she turns. That means to the side and to the rear, between her and the herd.

When you are driving a cow up the fence, stay back, but in her vision area. That way, she'll continue moving forward instead of turning away from the fence and trying to double back. When you are directly behind her, she will move forward, since she either hears you or senses your presence; but the pressure from the fence could cause her to turn away from it if you are not countering it and pushing her at the same time.

The herd instinct can be used to a penner's advantage.

This sequence of four photos shows the cutter with two cows out of the herd, but she doesn't want the cow on the left.

As the wrong-num-bered cow turns back to the herd, the rider speeds up to turn the other cow up the arena.

The herd holder on the Paint moves away from the fence to create an escape hole for the cow.

Success!

57

This rider is in good position to turn an unwanted cow back to the herd. She can easily see him, and he's no doubt yelling to make sure she knows he's out there. In a few more strides, he'll be far enough in front of her to turn her back. But if she happens to turn the wrong way, he's got enough room to maneuver and keep control of her. If this rider was driving the cow up the arena, he would be closer to her, and a little behind her.

When you are driving cattle, especially slow ones, don't get too close and override them. If you bump an animal, you could knock her to one side, turning her away from the direction you want her to go. You might also acquire a roughing call from one or both judges and receive a no-time.

But worse is the danger that the cow could fall down, or your horse could tangle his front legs in her back ones. In either case, you and your mount could crash to the ground. Riders have been seriously hurt in wrecks like this.

Always attempt to keep the cow's attention focused on you, rather than on a spectator across the fence, or on another cow. With her attention on you, she won't be thinking about returning to the herd, and you can control her. Without her attention, you are both in the arena at the same time, and that's about all.

Turning Cattle

Do this by placing yourself in a threatening position and exerting pressure so that the cow turns in the direction you want her to go. This can be done from some distance away. Move parallel to the cow, staying in her vision area and on the opposite side from the desired turn (figure C). By the time you reach her shoulder, the cow should be well aware of your presence and begin to fade away from you. Depending on how much turn you want, you can relax the pressure once action is initiated.

If you ride too far forward, up to a line with her eye, she'll stop first and then turn. If you ride on by, she'll sure stop, but she might turn in behind you. All of this depends on her vision area, and a penner should apply this knowledge.

Remember: Cattle turn *away* from a threat or pressure, and a rider is a threat. Cows will only turn into, or toward you,

This sequence of three photos shows a cutter riding hard to stay in the best position to turn a cow up the arena.

The turn-back riders have created an escape hole for the cow . . .

. . . and she moves between them. Once she spots the other cow already at the pen, she'll be easy for the turn-back rider on the left to move on up.

Always turn into the animal, not away.

when stronger pressure comes from another source (such as a turn-back rider in cutting) and she has no place else to go. By staying 20 to 30 feet away from her, you can maintain control and still be in position to counter any unwanted moves.

If you are right next to a cow, she can duck away, or stop and swing behind you, and you have no room or time to do anything about it. Watch the cow's head and ears. They will tell you when she is aware of your presence, which, in turn, means she will respond to your moves.

If the cutter and a turn-back rider are working together to ease a yearling out of the bunch, both must remember a cow's vision area and how she will respond to pressure and an opening for an escape. The turn-back rider has to spot the opening and then drop back, allowing the cow to escape from the cutter as soon as she is positioned to head down the arena.

Two riders trying to move a cow by "laning" her (riding parallel with the cow between them) won't get it done. They will only set her up so she can duck behind one rider, probably the cutter, since he's between her and the herd. The cow must always have an escape route from the cutter. The secret is for the turn-back rider to provide it in the direction that he wants the cow to go.

Stopping Cattle

Forward motion on a cow can be stopped from the side by going past her head and turning into her to make sure she turns away. Or, you can do it head-to-head as she comes at you. As always, you have to remember how cattle see and react.

When you are coming up alongside, staying in her vision area, ride by the shoulder and then to the eye. As you pass the eye, the cow will usually set up, stop, and turn directly away. Just make sure you are out where she can easily see you and be controlled. Of course, you have to stop and roll back into the cow, making sure that your horse faces her. Always turn *into* the animal, not away, since you will lose control if you are not facing toward the cow.

If you're out in the arena and want to aim the animal either toward the pen or back to the herd, jump right up to where you can push her in the desired direction. Unless a rider is careful at this point, he can easily lose contact, and control.

Sometimes when you want to stop a cow, you'll be riding stirrup to ribs, with the cow right against the fence. Go on by. She will stop, but because of the pressure from the fence, will probably turn behind

This penner, driving one up the fence, is in excellent position. He's staying back, but out to the side where the cow can see him. Although he's far enough back not to threaten the cow and make her turn, he's close enough to control her if she suddenly changes direction.

Keep the cow's attention on you. Notice how this yearling has turned her head ever so slightly to her right, and has dropped her right ear, indicating that she is watching the rider behind her.

61

This rider is turning the cow on the fence, and is doing a good job. She went by the cow, setting her up to turn back. She's also far enough away from the cow to have the space, and time, to roll back and keep control of the cow, and haze her up the fence. Notice that she's also rolling back toward the cow. When you turn away from a cow, you usually lose control of her.

you into the arena after you go by. Just try to regain your working advantage as quickly as possible.

In a head-to-head confrontation, try to give a little ground if possible. Remember the cow's blind spot for 10 to 15 feet in front of her. Giving ground tends to pull the cow to you, as well as allowing her time to stop. Then she can bend off in the direction of least resistance. A head-to-head situation most frequently takes place in the alley when you want to stop the cow's forward motion and then direct her toward the pen gate. As the alley rider, your job is to bluff the cow into stopping and then turning to the gate. Normally this works, but there are some cattle that nothing short of a high, solid wall will stop. They can slip around, behind, or even under a horse like a greased pig. Two almost sure signs that a cow is not going to stop: a lowered head and the tail up as she zeros in on where she wants to go.

The way that a cow reacts to your presence, along with the distance that she can be effectively worked from, results from several factors. Breeding, gentleness, age, how much she has been handled before the contest, the weather, and the number of times that she's been worked that day all determine how she will pen. A black baldy (Angus/Hereford cross) that has been around people before, and that has been penned several times already will usually require more pressure, but respond better, than a Brahma crossbred that's only seen a horse a few times. This is especially true if the latter has been jostled around in the trailer while being brought to the penning, and hasn't had time to settle down. When you work her, she will require lots of room, probably won't do what you expect her to do, and might push back pretty hard if not handled just right.

To summarize, you drive a cow while positioned directly behind her, or a little to one side while staying behind her hip. To turn her, position yourself opposite the area between her shoulder and eye. To stop her, go right on by and turn into her.

Working cattle on foot is an excellent way to learn how to handle them. Here, Jennifer Travis is approaching a cow and has her attention; note the position of the cow's head and ears.

As Jennifer continues walking forward, she crosses into the cow's vision area on her right side.

In a face-to-face situation, try to give a little ground and fill up all the alternatives so the cow has no place to go except where you want her to.

Here's an old cowboy expression worth remembering: *Never go where the cattle are; go where they're gonna be—otherwise you'll be too late.*

Also remember that when handling cattle, there's a time to move fast, and a time to move slow, and good cowboys know when to do both. This comes only from experience—from handling cattle yourself, or watching good cowboys handle cattle.

Working Cattle on Foot

The most effective way to learn how to control cattle, and understand how they react to your position, is to work a few on foot. It isn't as exciting as doing it horseback, but you will learn faster. If you're having to chase a cow all over, you'll quickly figure out the best way to control her with minimal effort on your part. The same methods you use on foot will apply when you are mounted.

Turn a gentle cow, yearling, or roping steer into a big corral or pen. Practice turning, stopping, and driving her. Apply

63

what you know about Ol' Bossy's vision, and how she reacts. Work slowly and quietly. That will give you time to analyze each move she makes. Before you know it, you'll be able to move her clear across the arena by taking just a few steps.

If you don't have the use of a gentle bovine, turn a horse loose in the pen and work him. He sees and reacts about the same way a cow does, and the experience will add to your savvy.

Once you've practiced on foot, try it horseback. Again, move slowly and quietly, especially if you are riding a horse that's inexperienced in handling cattle. He's got to learn to do things correctly at a slow pace before he can learn to do them correctly at a faster pace. If it's an older, experienced horse, he might not like the slow pace, but it will be good for him. It

As a result, the cow turns back the other way.

As the cow walks across the pen, so does Jennifer. As Jennifer gets into the cow's vision area, the cow stops, puts her attention on Jennifer . . .

. . . and then turns and goes the other way.

will help him to relax, stay quieter, and to watch the cow. When the cow stops, make the horse stop, stand, and not move until the cow does—or until you want to make her move. This will sharpen the skills of both you and your horse and will pay off at the next penning.

Some penners even use goats at home to help keep their horses alert and working. Because they are small and fast, goats can be harder to handle than cattle, and if a horse can control goats successfully, he sure ought to be able to handle cattle.

The cow moves some distance across the pen. Then Jennifer walks beyond the cow, and then toward her just a step or two . . .

. . . in order to turn the cow the other way. Then Jennifer sprints . . .

. . . to get into the cow's vision area to turn her once more.

9 SETTLING THE HERD

Team penning cattle are settled differently than are cattle used for cutting.

A FREQUENTLY overlooked, but very important, part of team penning is settling each herd of cattle brought into the arena. When settling is done properly, it allows every team working that set of cattle to have a fair chance. If the cattle are not settled, or if the settling is done poorly, the cattle will scatter like quail as soon as a cutter rides into the herd. This is especially true with the first team, but can also happen to subsequent teams.

The object of settling is to let the cattle get used to the arena and to a horse moving through them, and to honor (or respect) the turn-back riders. This makes each set of cattle as uniform as possible and gives each team a fair opportunity.

Cattle used for team penning are settled somewhat the same way that cutting cattle are—but with one big difference. With team penning cattle, the rider doing the settling always turns his horse *into* the cattle, instead of away from them. This acquaints the cattle with being driven, since they will move away from the horse turning into them. Driving cattle, of course, is the focal point of penning.

In settling cattle to be used for cutting, the settler always turns his horse away from them. This gets the cattle used to

Cattle must be settled properly to allow every team a fair chance.

This herd has just been brought into the arena, and several riders are holding them so they don't scatter up the arena.

After the cattle have calmed down, the settler begins riding back and forth in front of them, first at a walk, then a trot and lope.

The cattle start to scatter a little bit, but the settler trots ahead to turn them back.

In settling team penning cattle, the settler always turns toward the cattle, not away from them.

After the cattle accept the rider's presence, he slowly rides through them, all the way to the fence.

This starts the cattle moving up the arena.

But the herd holders roll them back. This is repeated several times until the cattle quietly flow around the rider. They are considered settled when they quietly move out of the horse's way, without trying to leave the bunch.

staying in a bunch, and accustomed to a horse working back and forth in front of them, with the horse's rump to the cattle. This also builds confidence in the cattle so they are less afraid of a horse in front of them. Then when a cow is cut out, she'll push hard at the cutter, trying to get back into the herd.

When the cattle first come into the arena, they will usually trot up the arena. If they do, the herd settler and his helpers ease the cattle back toward the gate and fence. Incidentally, the herd end of the arena should be the end where the cattle enter the arena. Then they will settle more quickly, and are more likely to remain at that end of the arena when being worked.

The riders give the cattle a few minutes to calm down. Then the settler will begin to ride back and forth across the arena, parallel to the herd and some distance from it. At first, he rides at a walk, then a trot, and finally at a lope.

As the cattle quiet down and accept his presence, he moves closer. Then he slowly rides into the herd, going clear to the back before he turns either right or left. This moves the cattle out and up the arena towards the herd holders, who roll them back into the bunch. The process is repeated a number of times, with the settler going in both directions, until the cattle are quiet and flow around him. The cattle are considered settled when they

When the cattle are settled, the action begins.

quietly move out of the horse's way without stampeding or trying to leave the bunch.

Depending on the type and breed of cattle, and their dispositions, settling can take from 5 to 30 minutes. Every herd is different, and it is up to the settler to determine when they are ready. One of the judges—usually the line judge—also shares in this decision.

The herd must also be resettled after each team works. For this job, a pair of herd holders ride into the arena. They gather up the cattle, and bunch them in the center of the arena, against the back fence. They make sure the cattle are in a compact group, with no stragglers off to one side and no drifters wandering up the arena. This normally takes only a few minutes.

While the herd holders are putting the herd back together, the next team rides into the arena and waits. When the herd holders and line judge are satisfied that the herd is bunched and ready, the judge raises his flag, the team springs into action, and the announcer calls out their designated number. While the team is galloping toward the herd, the herd holders lope out of the arena, leaving the field of action open for the penners.

10 MAKING A RUN

You can go into the herd quickly, but not so fast that the bunch explodes.

As soon as the first horse crosses the line, the flag drops and stopwatches start.

"THE CATTLE are ready, the flagger is ready, and . . . your number is FOUR!" blares the loudspeaker. Those words announce that your run has started, and that you and your teammates have 2 minutes to pen three head of shifty yearlings wearing the number 4.

There are three phases to a team penning run: cutting, moving the cattle up the arena, and penning them.

Cutting

During this phase, you must utilize everything you know about cattle—their eyesight, reactions, and speed—if your team is going to be successful. It is also the one part of the run when you should slow down rather than getting in too big a hurry and scattering cattle all over the arena. You can go into the herd quickly, but not so fast that the bunch explodes.

The most common approach is for one rider to enter the herd while his teammates stay back, one on each side of the arena (Figure A). This way, the turn-back riders can roll the cattle back to the center instead of letting them drift up the fence, as the cutter pushes his selected animals out of the herd.

Sometimes, one team member cuts out all three head. At other times, one rider will cut first, and while he drives a cow out, another teammate is already entering

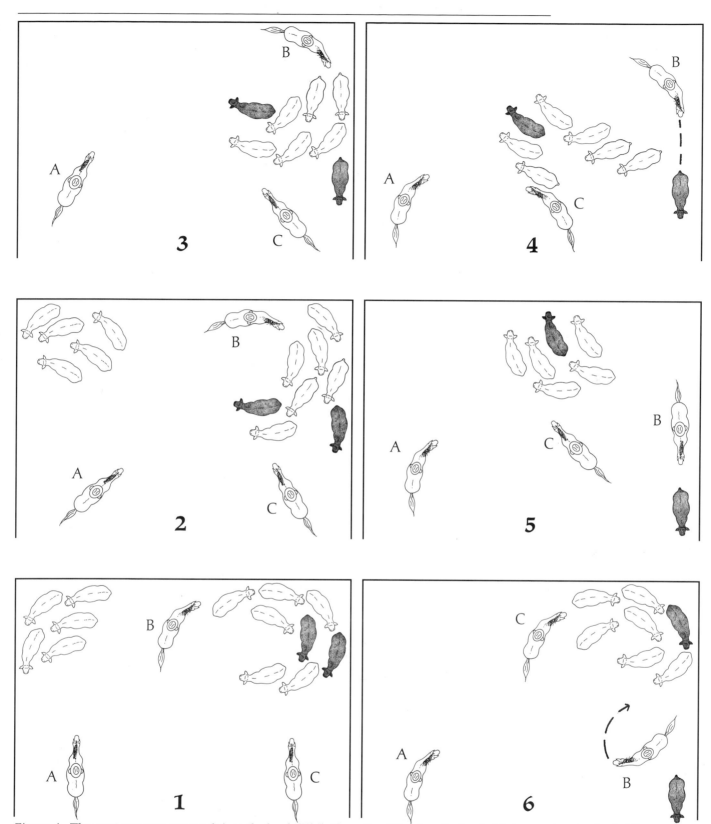

Figure A. The most common approach into the herd. While the cutter (B) enters the herd, his teammates stay back. The cutter has spotted two cows (shaded ones) on his right that he wants (1). As the cattle come up the fence, the turn-back rider (C) rolls them back, and also moves up to create an escape hole for one of the wanted cows (2) & (3). The cutter brings that cow right up the fence (4), while the turn-back rider goes after the other cow (5). As that rider brings the cow up the fence, the first cutter (B) will turn his horse and help move the second cow up the arena (6).

Usually, the cutter splits the herd and goes all the way to the back fence before turning. This opens the herd up, making it easier to spot numbers.

The turn-back rider is positioned to roll the cattle back as the cutter waits for the opportunity to cut out the cow he wants.

the herd to cut out another cow. This tactic can be selected in advance, or can be an on-the-spot decision, depending on the circumstances. Penners must adapt to the way the cattle are handling, and where their cattle are, to be effective. For example, if a turn-back rider sees a cow that he can easily get, he should push her out after the cutter has safely cleared the herd with his cow. Then the cutter becomes a turn-back rider.

Sometimes when the cutter goes into the herd, the cattle will split unevenly, with most of them on one side and just a few on the other. In this situation, if none of the desired cattle are on the "weak side," the turn-back man on that side will move up to help the cutter. He doesn't cut any out, but positions himself to break up the mass of cattle so it's easier for the cutter to work. His presence applies pressure and helps to move the cattle so they can't bunch up.

This is similar to the situation when cattle are being counted through a gate. To prevent a bunch of cattle from all

Here's another photo showing how the cattle are rolling out and around the cutter as he tries to push out one of his cows.

trying to go through the gate at the same time, one rider will position himself in front of the gate and slightly to one side to break up the cattle and slow them down.

There's still another method of cutting called the "shotgun." In this style, the riders agree in advance to go into the herd one right after the other, just as soon as the preceding cutter has cleared the herd. Even though the order of cutting is agreed upon in advance, the team must be flexible enough to alter the plan when necessary. For example, sometimes there will be one or two head off to one side where the person who was to cut last can collect them immediately. These cattle take first priority, but that rider must let his partners know by shouting, "I've got two right here!"

In certain situations—such as when the cattle are gentle and will stick together, or in an all-or-nothing situation—two cutters will go into the herd simultaneously, entering from the sides, not the center. This method leaves only one turn-back rider to keep the herd from scattering up the arena.

If the first two cutters get their cows out, they hold herd while the third rider goes into the herd after the remaining cow. When this method works, the time can be spectacular. But more often than not, it means that cattle escape across the foul line.

In rare situations, all three riders will attack the herd at the same time, with each rider zeroing in on a specific animal. One rider will hold back slightly to allow a teammate to move a cow out of the herd and toward the pen. In essence he is a turn-back rider, but is close enough to the herd where he can move in as soon as there is an opening. Again, when this tactic works, the time can be sensational; but just as often, the cattle will stampede across the foul line for a no-time.

There are usually only two occasions when a team will use this method. The first: When it's their only hope of beating a team, or teams, that have already established excellent times.

The second: When the arena is so large that it will allow the team to "regroup" and turn the herd back before it reaches the foul line.

In certain situations, two cutters will go into the herd simultaneously.

75

This sequence of five photos shows the team-work between the cutter and turn-back riders, and how the latter have to change position as the situation changes. In the first photo, they are staying back, giving the cutter room to work the cattle, yet close enough to move in and help if necessary.

The cutter has isolated the cow he wants, but she decides to rejoin her buddies.

Both cow and cutter head for the fence. Notice how the horse is fading away from the cow. This will put him in better position to block the cow when they reach the fence. If he's right next to her, she's more apt to run under his neck, or cut back and run behind him. Also notice how the turn-back rider on the right is starting to move away from the fence, because he knows the cutter will bring the cow up the fence.

The cutter gets the cow blocked and turned, and the turn-back rider has moved over to create an opening for her.

Then the turn-back rider jumps up to help drive the cow farther away from the herd.

A team's strategy in cutting must be adapted to the type and wildness of the cattle, the size of the arena, and the times already made. Sometimes it's better to play it safe by keeping the cattle under control and getting all three head penned—albeit in a slower time—rather than risking everything for a sizzling time. This is especially true when you're going for the average. At other times, all a team can do is go for broke and hope that it works.

Regardless of the style of cutting, the first cutter should be scanning the herd for his numbers as he approaches it. And by the time he's at the herd, he should have spotted at least one of his cows. But, his teammates should help him. It's surprising how difficult it can be to spot your number in a herd of milling cattle, especially when you are working against the clock.

A teammate might yell, "Bald-faced brindle to your left and facing you, halfway back." Translated, this means that a white-faced brown cow with dark stripes is on the cutter's left and about halfway through the herd to the back fence. Then it's up to the cutter to ease her out so a turn-back rider can send her up the arena. Penners have got to talk to one another. It pays off in faster times.

77

All three riders are working together here. The cutter has separated the wanted cow (darker one) from her partner, and will push her between the two turn-back riders. The rider on the left is turning to push the unwanted cow back to the herd. The other rider is the one who rolled the two cows across the arena; she will now hold up, leaving an escape hole for the wanted cow.

Normally, the cutter will enter the herd about in the middle and go all the way to the back fence before turning right or left. This splits the herd, opening it up and making it easier to spot numbers and push out the one(s) the cutter wants. Which way he turns will depend on whether he has seen any of his numbers. If he sees one or two on his right, he'll turn right.

When the cutter has cattle moving away from the back fence and up the side fence, he might have the opportunity to separate one of the assigned cows. If the cow is in front of other cows, the turn-back rider can move back, leaving a hole through which the cow can escape, then jump in to roll the other cows to the center. As the turn-back rider creates the hole, the cutter has to slack off his pressure, letting the cattle slow down so the unwanted cattle don't shove on through the hole with the wanted cow. Once that cow is out by herself, and the turn-back rider has turned the trash back, he (turn-back rider) should apply enough pressure on her to send her on up the arena.

If the desired animal can't be separated along the fence, the turn-back rider will roll the bunch towards the center. Both he and the cutter must work as a team, moving the cattle back and forth across the arena, dropping off trash each pass until the quarry can be separated. The cutter applies the pressure and the turn-back rider supports him, pushing when all the cattle are grouped and, when the opportunity arises, giving ground to make the opening that a wanted cow can escape through, and blocking the un-wanted ones. The riders *must* work as a team, anticipating what the cow will do and then giving her the alternative of moving in the right direction.

As the cutter pushes the cattle toward the turn-back riders, the latter must be careful to give the cattle enough room to come up the arena. This allows the cutter some working space and lets the animals move away from him. If the whole bunch is jammed up against the back fence, the cattle will mill around in a tight mass and the cutter can't do his job. Cattle must see

These two photos show two riders in the herd at the same time, which can be done when the cattle stick together. The one turn-back rider is already moving to make sure the small bunch in front of the palomino turns back.

The palomino's rider got one cow cut out . . . but didn't get her far enough away from the herd before she turned back. Meanwhile, the other rider in the herd has spotted a cow he wants. This team's run is starting to fall apart here.

a threat (the cutter) in order to react, and that means they must have space between themselves and the rider.

When Lady Luck is riding with a team, one of their cows will be off to one side all by herself, or maybe with just one or two other cows. This "sitting duck" should be the first target. The cutter, or the turn-back rider on that side, should slip between the "duck" and the herd, separate her, and start her up the arena. This cow will become bait for the others, giving them one to go to. Because cattle are herd animals, once you get two or more together, they will handle much better than they will singly.

The position of the "duck" determines your approach. Dashing in at the wrong angle will often turn her *into* the herd.

But, a rider who suddenly appears between the "duck" and the herd will often squirt her into the open. Then the turn-back rider can move out of the way to provide an escape route (Figure B).

Turn-back riders. These riders have two jobs. One is to contain the herd, rolling the cattle back toward the center of the pen, so the cutter can do his job. The second is to help cut out a cow when the opportunity arises. They do this by creating an opening through which the cow can escape when the cutter applies pressure.

Frequently, the turn-back rider must juggle both jobs at the same time, and handle several head going in different

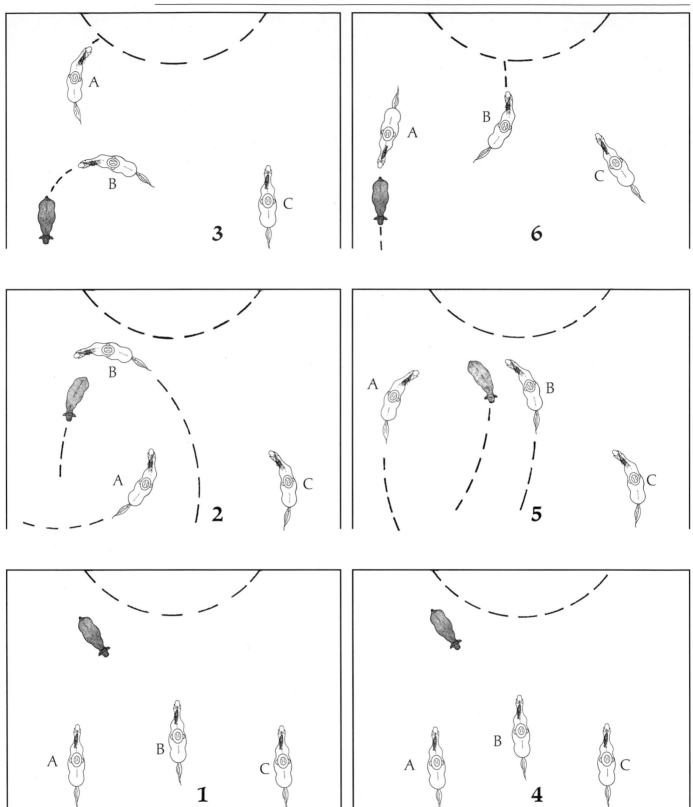

Figure B. Two different ways to handle a "sitting duck." Sequence 1, 2, and 3 shows the cutter (B) bringing the duck out, and the turn-back rider (A) going into the herd after the next cow. Sequence 4, 5, and 6 shows how the turn-back rider can bring the duck out, with help from the cutter (B), who then continues into the herd.

As this rider peels one cow away from the herd and heads her up the fence, a teammate moves in to get their next cow.

directions. That's when the cutter must be aware of the turn-back rider's situation, hold up, and let the cattle head back to the herd rather than risk shoving them over the turn-back rider and across the foul line. It's in situations like this when the real teamwork becomes obvious.

Some penners have developed a real ability at turning back and habitually work that position. They have the knowledge to read cattle, can see situations developing, and are able to counter them. They understand teamwork and, as a rule, are extremely well-mounted. Sometimes they have to go down the fence at a dead run to split a pair of yearlings, or to turn a bunch quitter back to the herd, or to prevent a yearling already cut out from rejoining the herd.

In addition to helping the cutter, rolling the herd back, keeping drifters from crossing the foul line, and breaking up pairs and triples, the turn-back riders must always know where the worked cattle are. Keeping one from returning to the herd is just as important as getting it out in the first place.

All three penners must always know where their partners are, too. Turning a yearling in front of another rider cannot only spoil the run, but cause a wreck as

well. More than one horse has gone down after colliding with a cow. Riders can also collide with each other—with disastrous results. Team penning is a fast sport, one that combines 30 head of cattle, 3 horses, and 3 riders. Accidents can happen quickly if the riders aren't watching what they are doing, where they are going, and where their teammates are.

Moving Up the Arena

Once the three designated cows are cut out and moved away from the herd, the team should group them as rapidly as possible. Cattle always work better in a bunch, as we have said before. Be careful, however, not to crowd them so much that they scatter. Move them as quickly as possible, but at a speed that can be controlled. Some yearlings run faster than others. Some, if they are tired, just lope along or even trot. Penners must recognize what the animals will do and adapt to it. More than one run has been blown at this stage because a rider got too anxious and couldn't stay back off of the cattle.

All three penners must always know where their partners are.

While the turn-back rider gallops to the fence to turn the trash back, the cutter moves up to separate the Hereford he wants from the light-colored cow.

This cutter wants the Hereford on the far left, but if he doesn't get his ol' pony turned in a hurry, she's going to get by him.

The riders should stay lined up across the arena as they push the cows, making sure that they don't leave an opening for one to turn back through. If one person is too far up, or too far back, the pressure is uneven and one of the cows could react by heading back to the herd. If you're going to pen them, you've got to control them.

Like pool, team penning is a game of position. The cattle are the balls, the arena fence is the table side (and cattle can be "banked" off the side for position), and riders apply the pressure that puts the cattle where they want them. Too much pressure from the wrong direction, and the cattle move out of position and the team loses control.

Penning the Cattle

After the cattle pass the back of the pen, the rider on the side of the arena closest to the pen veers off and heads for the alley. That rider automatically becomes the alley or in-the-hole rider. The rider in the middle automatically becomes the wing man, while the remaining rider automatically becomes the swing rider. Assuming the positions automatically eliminates any confusion as to who goes where and prevents any gaps from opening up in the line as the cattle are hazed to the top of the arena.

To eliminate confusion, let's assume that the pen is on the right side of the arena; that is, on the riders' right as they bring the cattle up the arena.

Smart penners use the fence just as if it were another rider. After stopping both cows from going up the fence, the turn-back rider moves to create an opening for the wanted cow (the one next to the fence).

With the fence on her right and the cutter pressuring her from behind, the cow heads up the fence toward the other cows in the background. Meanwhile, the turn-back rider pushes the unwanted cow back to the herd.

Another example of using the fence. The rider behind is pushing the cow, yet is slightly out to the side where the cow can see him. The other rider is far enough away, and is holding up so her presence doesn't cause the cow to turn back. The fence keeps the cow running straight.

This rider is in hot pursuit of a cow that escaped from the pen end of the arena. If she can get ahead of the cow, she might be able to turn her back since the cow is not right next to the fence and there is room for the cow to reverse directions by turning into the fence.

This cutter has sorted out two of his cows (No. 9), but has also picked up an extra. He has pressured the No. 9 cow on the right to move her away from the herd.

Now he's pulled up to push the second one out; hopefully the unwanted cow on the left will drop back. This is a neat bit of work that will shave seconds off his team's time. If it's necessary, a turn-back rider can move in to make sure the No. 9 on the right doesn't go back to the herd.

Be ready to change position when the situation requires it. In this case, while the first cutter is moving a cow up the arena, a teammate heads for the herd to get their second cow.

It's a lot easier to push your second and third cows out when they can see the first cow. In this photo, the team's second cow heads for the first one, while the cutter turns back to get the third cow. The turn-back rider had moved away from the fence to create an escape hole for the cow . . . and is now watching the unwanted cow to make sure she goes back to the herd.

As the cattle pass the end of the wing, the swing rider moves up and puts a little pressure on the right side of the bunch to angle them to the right—toward the arena fence, and then brings them along the fence, toward the gate of the pen. He must maintain the cows' forward momentum, but not crowd them so much that the little bunch splits, turns back, or tries to escape down the alley.

Meanwhile, the rider in the middle has pulled up slightly beyond the end of the wing. His job is to assist the swing rider, pushing the cattle to the top of the arena, and blocking any attempts they might make to double back. He functions as a mobile extension of the wing.

The timing of the alley or the hole rider is critical. If he breaks off for the alley too soon, he might create an opening for the cattle to escape through—back down the arena. But if he waits too long, he might not be in position when the cattle swing around the top of the arena and head for the pen.

When he first rides into the alley, he should position himself three-quarters of the way up the alley. Then as the cattle come around the top of the arena, the alley rider should move to the top of the alley. If he goes there initially, when the cattle do come around the top of the arena, he will probably move too far up, either turning the cattle too soon, pushing

If both turn-back riders get busy at the top end of the arena and the cutter puts too much pressure on the herd, they might spill across the foul line. That's going to happen here if a turn-back rider doesn't spot the problem and hustle back.

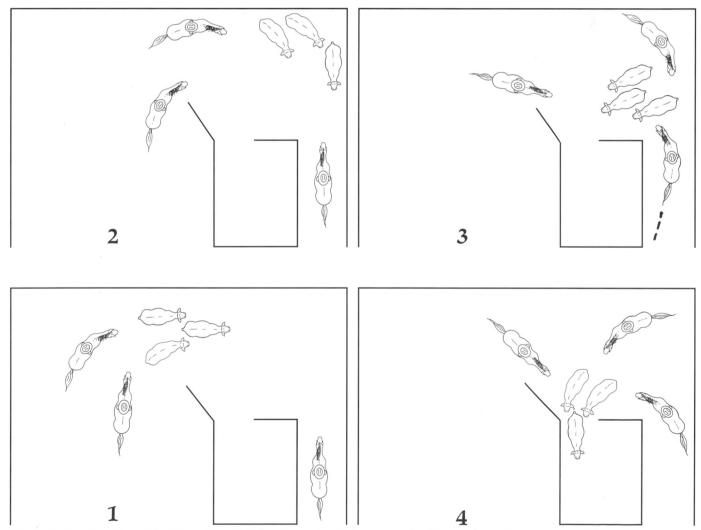

Figure C. Penning the cattle. When the hole rider first enters the alley, he should stop about three-quarters of the way up the alley (1). Then as the cattle come around the top of the arena, he can move up and push them toward the gate (2, 3, & 4).

As riders take their cattle up the arena, they should stay in a straight line. If a rider is too far forward, or too far back, it creates a hole that a cow can escape through.

As the cows pass the back end of the pen, the rider closest to the alley peels off to ride into it. The rider in the middle becomes the wing man, while the one on the right becomes the swing rider.

At this point, the hole rider holds up before reaching the top of the alley. If he moves there too soon, he might turn the cattle back, or push them over the wing rider.

As the swing rider brings the cattle around, along the fence, the hole rider moves up to turn them toward the gate. The wing rider should actually be farther away from the gate—at the end of the wing . . .

. . . but in this case, it didn't cause a problem.

This sequence of three photos shows what can happen when riders are not in a straight line. Because the rider on the left is so far ahead, a big hole opens.

The wing rider helps to funnel the cattle into the gate.

one or more of them over the wing man, or creating an escape hole in the alley. So he should stay back in the alley when he first rides into it (Figure C).

As the cattle come around the top of the arena and the alley rider moves up, his job is to turn them toward the pen gate and keep their momentum going. If they stall out now, they may turn or try to break past the wing rider.

Once the alley rider turns the cattle off the fence and toward the gate, the swing rider increases the pressure on them. He should be positioned about 45 degrees to the rear and side of the bunch where he can still drive them, but jump forward to help the wing man stop any escape attempts.

The wing rider stays close to the end of the wing, helping to funnel the cattle into the gate.

Because of the pressure from all three riders, the only escape route for the cattle is into the gate. As the last cow goes in, one or more riders should spur in behind her, raising an arm to signal that the run is complete.

That's the way things are supposed to go. But, they don't always happen that way.

Calling for time. The judge drops his flag when one or more penners rides into the gate and raises an arm. The flag will drop when the nose of the first horse goes through the gate. However, time will continue until any extra cattle on the pen side of the start/foul line are punched back across the line to the herd.

Usually it will be just one extra cow, because the team would already have been flagged out if they had four or

A cow spots it . . .

. . . and heads back toward the herd.

In a large arena, bringing the cattle around the top of the arena alongside the fence is a safe way to maintain control of them, but it takes up valuable time. Not only is this team taking the long way around, they've got an extra critter.

This team is shaving seconds off their time by turning their cattle toward the pen before they reach the fence. The swing rider does this by moving out to the right side of the cattle.

The hole rider is in position (in front of the flag judge) and is waving an arm and probably hollering to direct the cattle into the gate.

The wing rider gallops into the pen right behind the cattle and the flag drops. This sequence of pictures shows the type of run all penners hope for when they bring their cattle up the arena.

For whatever reason, this hole man is far too late and the cattle could stampede right up the alley.

These two pictures show good teamwork at the pen. As the swing man brings the cattle around, the hole man rides out of the alley to turn them toward the gate. The wing man is positioned to stop them from going by the wing; he can move forward or back as needed.

And the cattle funnel right into the pen.

As the cattle come around the top of the arena and head for the gate, it's important to keep them moving at a steady pace. If they are going too slowly, one or two might stop or turn off. If they are going too fast, they could stampede down the alley. Keep even pressure on the cattle.

more across the line. But sometimes, for example, a team might decide to call for time with only two correct cows in the pen. The extras must be pushed back across the line before time stops.

If one of the correct cows escapes from the pen before all the unpenned cattle are driven across the start/foul line, it is an automatic no-time. The same is true if a team calls "time" with a wrong-numbered animal in the pen.

As mentioned in the chapter on rules, rules do vary between associations. In at least one association, calling for time before all of the unpenned cattle are back across the start/foul line will result in a no-time. And at some pennings, the team must shut the gate before time stops. So know the rules for the penning where you are competing.

One last thing about calling time. The judge will not drop his flag until one of the team members rides to the gate and raises a hand. More than one penner has ridden to the gate, held the cattle, and then just sat there with both hands on the saddle horn as the seconds tick by. Don't be bashful; stick your arm up in the air!

95

11 PROBLEMS

Sometimes it's faster to push both animals back into the herd and start over.

DESPITE HOW skilled a team might be, things can go wrong in a hurry in a penning run. Let's look at some of them, starting with an extra cow that comes out of the herd with the cow you want. Use what you know about how cattle see and react, and try the following tactics.

When the wanted cow is out in front, along the fence, and has some lead on the second cow, the turn-back rider can angle in at the hip of the wanted cow; he should move in fast to push her on and stop the second one. The sudden pressure from behind should squirt the first cow forward where she can be pushed on toward the pen, and stop and turn the unwanted cow back into the herd.

Suppose the two cows are going up the fence, but are overlapped with the wanted cow behind the first one and closest to the fence. The turn-back rider should move in from the front, stopping and turning the two animals toward the center of the arena. He will apply most of the pressure on the first cow, hopefully splitting the pair apart and slowing the second one. As he moves after the first one, he leaves an opening that the wanted cow can take to go up the fence. The cutter should move up between that cow and the herd, applying pressure to send her on up the arena. The turn-back rider will push the extra animal back to the herd.

If the two cows persist in staying together, the cutter and the turn-back rider will have to work the animals back and forth until the opportunity arises to split off the wanted one. Often, the two animals will stick so close together they can't be split on their first pass across the arena.

The cutter wants the black baldy (No. 5) and not the Herefords, which are already turning back to the herd. If she can spur up just a little, she can turn No. 5 up the arena, while the Herefords lope back to the herd.

This rider had one extra cow, but managed to gallop between them and send the unwanted cow (out of view behind his horse) back to the herd and the wanted cow toward the pen.

This team has got one extra cow, and although it's difficult to tell which critter is the trash, it looks like both cows will squirt between the two riders and head up the arena. Sometimes when the action is this fast, it's tough for the riders to reposition themselves to prevent something like this from happening.

Then, it may be faster to push them back into the herd and start over again.

Sometimes the cow that you want will be directly behind another one. In this case, pushing will send both of them across the foul line. Therefore, the turn-back rider must get in front of the two animals, stopping and turning them across the arena. As they turn, the cutter should move up and apply pressure on the first one. Hopefully, as he pushes the first cow across the arena, the second (wanted) cow will slow down. If this happens, the turn-back rider should take advantage of the opening created and move in and around to turn the second cow up the arena.

He must be careful at this point to split the two and let *only the wanted cow* move up the arena, while the extra goes back to the herd.

When the two animals won't split, they should be worked across the arena until the wanted cow can be cut off and the extra returned to the herd. Again, it may be faster to push both animals back into the herd and start over.

Two extras. When the wanted cow is in front, going up the fence, treat the

97

This cutter is coming out with one extra, and it looks like it's No. 3, the cow closest to the camera. If so, the turn-back rider is galloping over to create an escape hole for the wanted cow and also to turn back the extra. Meanwhile, the cutter should spur up more to the left of the wanted cow so she doesn't follow the extra back to the herd.

1/ In this situation, the wanted cow is in front, while the two behind are extras. The rider turns a little to his right as he rides toward them.

2/ This stops the two extras, giving the rider an opening.

3/ He can now haze the wanted cow up the arena, while the two extras will return to the herd.

1/ Here's a sequence of four pictures showing the wanted cow on the fence, in front (partially hidden behind rider). The cutter does not want the light-colored cow, so lets her follow the herd.

2/ The wanted cow can't decide whether to follow the light-colored cow, or turn back on the fence. The cutter, anticipating that she will turn back on the fence, starts turning his horse to get between her and the cow behind her.

3/ Just as the cow starts to turn back, the rider jumps over to block her.

4/ He gets her stopped, and will now position himself to take her up the fence. Meanwhile, the turn-back rider will have moved over to create an escape hole for her on the fence.

1/ This cutter has two extras, but jumps up to get between them and the light-colored cow that he wants.

If you can't split the cattle along the fence, turn them back to the center of the arena.

situation as you would with a single extra. The turn-back rider should come in at an angle, slip behind the correct cow to push her on up the arena and turn the two delinquents back.

Suppose the cow you want is between the two extras, as they are all going up the fence single file. In this case, stop, turn, and drop off the first one, trying to leave an escape hole up the fence for the correct cow. Then close in and try to turn the third cow back to the herd.

If the cow you want is behind two extras, get in front of all of them to block their progress. Then try to turn the first two back to the herd while leaving an opening for the wanted cow to continue up the arena.

If you aren't able to quickly split the cattle along the fence, turn them back to the center of the arena. Yell for help and, with a teammate, work them back and forth until you have the one you want. Be careful that you don't get in too big a hurry and scatter your cattle. Work only as fast as they'll let you.

Also remember that the distance from the herd to the foul line isn't too far in most cases. So if you're getting worried that too many cattle are getting too close to the foul line, turn 'em all back and yell for help.

More than three extras. Go to the center with them and work back and forth until you have cut the trash off. Keeping track of four, five, or more yearlings is tricky, and you don't want to give them room to sneak past you and cross the foul line. Sometimes it's better to even let the bunch back into the herd and start over, rather than taking a chance with too many getting over the foul line.

Trash at the top. Often there is no way to prevent extra critters from joining a buddy at the top (pen end) of the arena. That means the trash must be cut out and sent back to the herd. Be sure and tell your partners that you already have an extra cow or two across the line so they don't send more cattle, resulting in a no-time.

You can work the cattle at the top of the arena along the fence or back and forth

2/ He gets her out in the middle by herself, but before he can get her turned to go up the arena . . .

3/ . . . she sucks back to follow her buddies. Unless the rider can roll back and block her, she's gone. This is a good example of why a team penner, to be successful, needs a horse with cow sense that can also handle.

This is an example of pure chaos, which can happen when the herd starts scattering and the riders don't work as a team. In a situation like this, it's usually best to regroup and start over.

across the arena to sort out the trash and head them back to the herd. Depending on where you get them cut out, you can head them straight down the arena, or even down the alley, between the pen and the arena fence. Just get them out of there quickly . . . and make sure the wanted cow(s) stay at the pen end.

Cattle in the alley. Cattle will not always go straight up the arena, and it's not unusual for a cow or two, or maybe all three, to go up the fence in the alley. This is okay. If there are two, push them on through so they join up with the third one. If it's just one, push her so she joins her buddies at the top of the arena. If all three go up the alley, do not push them so far that you take them all the way around the top of the arena, going beyond the pen. The alley rider should slow down, and wait for the wing man and swing rider to get in position so the cattle can be hazed right into the pen.

Cattle already cut. These cattle can be a problem in that often they want to return to the herd. This is especially true if you've only got one across the line. The turn-back riders have to watch these cows, because it's a costly mistake if one (or more) gets back into the herd.

If you've got two across the line, get them together as quickly as possible because they will be more likely to stay put. The turn-back riders still have to watch them, however, because both might decide to rejoin the herd. If these lonesome cows (or cow) get a head start, they can be pretty hard to turn. The trick is to get them stopped before they build up any speed.

This is one part of penning where spectators can help by calling out a warning when they see cows heading back to the herd. But by the time a turn-back rider realizes it and gets his horse turned around, it might be too late.

If the cattle cannot be separated along the fence or if you have more than three extras, roll them across the arena and work them back and forth until you get the wanted cows cut out.

If a cow has started back, and is still walking or just jogging, she can usually be turned back if the rider can get in position to present a threat. But once she has dropped her head, raised her tail, and shifted into high gear, she probably won't pay any attention to the horse and rider.

Turning away from the pen. Often a team will have their cows almost to the top of the arena when the critters will turn away from the pen. There are usually reasons for this, even though cattle can be unpredictable.

One reason (let's assume the pen is on the riders' right): Possibly the middle rider moved too far forward, applied pressure, and caused the cattle to turn back to the left.

Another reason: Possibly the swing rider was too far to the right and inadvertently caused pressure that turned the cattle back to the left. Or maybe either the swing rider or wing rider were crowding the cattle and they split to the left.

Still another reason: Maybe there was an extra cow at the pen end of the arena. If she happens to be heading to the left when your three head arrive, they might decide to join up with her.

Regardless of the reason that the cattle head the wrong way, the swing and wing riders have to double back, get around the bunch, and point them in the desired direction. If there's an extra critter, she'll have to be cut out. Sometimes the best way is to isolate her on the right, shove her down the alley, and back across the line.

If there isn't an extra cow, both riders can bring the cattle up as before, and make the swing to the right. It might mean a reshuffling of positions between the wing and swing riders, but if it gets the cattle in position, it makes no difference.

105

1/ In this sequence, the rider has two cows that she wants in front, but an extra on the fence. She gets the extra stopped . . .

Cattle that have turned away from the gate once will be twice as hard to pen the next time.

Scattering at the top. Some cattle just won't bunch up and, if you're unlucky enough to draw three like that, you have problems. Generally you will realize they aren't going to bunch as you bring them up the arena; so as you approach the top of the arena, keep them moving, but take it easy. If independent-type cattle are crowded too much, they'll scatter, so don't rush; and work with your teammates to block each cow as she tries to escape. Don't leave any holes.

Sometimes nothing will hold cattle like this in a small group, and the run falls apart.

A penner can tell when cattle aren't going to bunch up, or stay bunched. They'll all be looking in different directions, won't show that they're tuned in on the same wavelength as far as movement is concerned, and are trying to circle off instead of traveling together. When you spot these signs, tell your team members and get ready for action.

Once the cows have moved past the wing and are circling the top of the arena, the alley rider has to watch closely, making sure the animals know he is there and can block them. He should, however, stay slightly back until the time comes to "spook" them toward the gate.

Both the swing and wing riders have to cover more ground with cattle apt to split and run. They have to keep them moving, closing up tempting holes, but not putting on so much pressure that the little group explodes in three directions. Sometimes, they get almost to the gate when the strange pen turns them back. Other times . . . who knows? When they do scatter, the riders have to do their best to regroup them, changing positions if necessary, and try to bring them back up. Cattle that have turned away from the gate once will be twice as hard to pen the next time.

2/ . . . and turns her back . . .

3/ . . . but she's determined to follow her buddies. The rider needs to get turned and gallop up to send the cow back to the herd, or have a turn-back rider help turn the cow.

Here's some good teamwork between the cutter and turn-back rider to get a cow separated from the bunch while they were rolling across the arena. If the spotted cow follows the wanted cow, the riders will have to cut her back.

These riders have just nailed their third cow and are ready to head up the arena while the extra lopes back to the herd.

108

1/ This team wants the No. 2 cow, the Hereford closest to the rider in the background.

2/ The cutter gets her turned up the arena— but several extras tag along.

3/ When the trash turns back, No. 2 also turns back, and is now on the fence. The rider in front is reining out to his right, hoping to get in front of her and turn her before she reaches the herd. Meanwhile, another No. 2 already sent up the arena waits for company.

The line judge (lower left) is just about ready to flag this team out for having too many cattle across the line. There are already two on the left, two in front of the rider, and a bunch more coming up fast. The imaginary foul line runs between the judge and the flag above the No. 4 chute.

Here are three cows headed in different directions as they approach the top end of the arena. This is not a good situation. When this happens, team members have to rely on their cow savvy and skill to get the cows bunched and all headed in the correct direction.

110

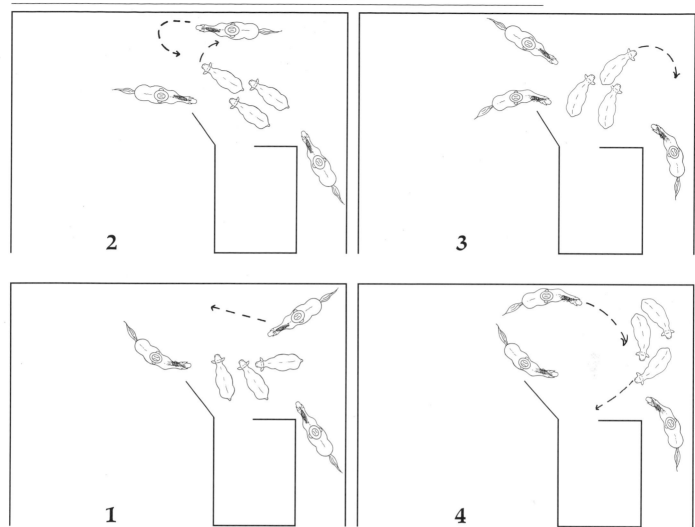

Figure A. If more than one cow is trying to escape around the wing (No. 1), the swing rider should move over to help the wing rider (No. 2). The wing rider can move away from the wing a short distance, but not far enough to create an escape hole. As the cattle turn away from the wing (No. 3), the hole rider and swing rider funnel them back toward the gate (No. 4).

Going down the alley. Some cows come around the top of the arena with a head of steam built up and don't have turn on their mind as they head for the alley. A horse in the way isn't going to stop them, no matter how much the rider moves around, waves his arm, and yells. Remember the cow's blind spot out in front? Sometimes the cow doesn't see the horse and rider and just keeps coming.

Ordinarily, the alley rider should move up as the cattle come off the back fence, turning them toward the gate. He should stay in the center of the alley, moving his horse from side to side to fill the space. Turning sideways is usually a mistake since the rider loses visual contact with a cow if she heads for the horse's rear—and because a cow can easily slip behind the horse before the rider can get turned around. Even backing up won't stop some yearlings. Sometimes a cow will even run under a horse's neck. So it's best to always face the cattle.

The secret of handling the alley is intimidation; but even so, some cattle won't pay any attention to the alley rider.

Going around the wing. While blocking a cow trying to get past the wing is the primary responsibility of the rider stationed there, the swing rider can also help. If more than one animal is trying to make a dash around the wing, two riders can seal off the opening better than one. The

111

1/ *This is what can happen when a hole opens up in the line of riders bringing the cattle up the arena . . . or when a cow simply decides she's going back to the herd. The rider in the middle breaks off to turn her back . . .*

2/ *. . . and he gets the job done, but she tries it again alongside the fence, and the other two are thinking of joining her.*

3/ Once cattle start scattering, it can be hard to get them bunched again, but this team seems to have things under control now.

wing rider must move away from the wing toward the top of the arena, but not so far that he leaves a big hole. He must always remember that he functions as an extension of the wing.

The swing rider should come across the top of the arena, between the cattle and the arena fence, until he can get in front of the animals (see figure A). That puts two riders on that side of the arena with only the alley rider covering the far side of the pen, and he must always be in position to block the alley. Once the cattle are stopped and are circling back, the swing rider will move back into position, re-group the cattle, and attempt to push them toward the gate. The danger here is that the cattle will turn back from the wing rider and then try the alley.

Frequently, the wing rider can face down a single cow by moving his horse at her, yelling and waving an arm. Other times, nothing will stop one from going on by. The wing rider must guard against moving in too quickly when the cattle are headed toward the gate and responding to the pressure from the swing rider behind

them. His presence, or just a step or two forward, is usually enough to turn them into the gate. If he does move up too much, he can turn the cattle back on the swing rider. The pressure from behind, plus that coming from the wing, can cause the animals to set and scatter.

Cattle that try to get between the end of the wing and the wing rider can often bring on a roughing call. Depending upon where the rider is positioned, the space can be small—and gets smaller as the rider moves in to close it off. The cow and the rider are both moving rapidly, and a collision often occurs with the horse knocking the cow into the wing. If that happens, it's roughing and a no-time.

Turning back at the gate. The usual reason for this: the alley rider moving up too fast, trying to make sure he gets through the gate right after the cattle to raise his hand. He applies pressure on his side of the cows and causes them to veer

Sometimes when the wing rider moves up too fast, he can turn the cattle back on the swing rider.

1/ If you have an extra cow as you approach the top of the arena and can't get her turned back on the fence . . .

2/ . . . one solution is to follow her all the way around the pen . . .

114

to the opposite side. Give them time to make that turn through the gate before moving in.

This isn't the only reason that cattle will turn back at the gate. Sometimes, the wing or swing rider comes up too quickly, adding too much pressure to cows not moving as fast as the horses. Although the gate is an escape opening, the animals hesitate, feel too much pressure, and scatter. Then again, cattle don't always need a reason for what they do.

When the animals do split and scatter at the gate, the team should regroup them as rapidly as possible. If the cattle stay at the top end of the arena, sometimes this can be done by the three riders holding their places and giving the cattle time to settle before trying to pen them again. But if the cattle scatter through the wing and swing riders, and head back toward the herd,

that means a horse race for all three penners. If possible, gather them, throw them into a group, and try again. If it doesn't work . . . that's penning luck.

Four across the line. Since the rules do allow four head across the line, a team sometimes has an extra near the pen. They should cut it off, pen their three assigned head and then two team members stay in the gate, holding the cattle, while their partner drives the extra animal across the line. When the extra animal crosses the line, the judge's flag will fall, signaling time.

Trash in the pen. Sooner or later a team will pen four head instead of just three. That extra cow must be cut out and driven back across the foul line before time can

Sooner or later a team will pen four head instead of just three.

115

1/ Here's a team with four head at the top of the arena.

2/ The alley rider blocks the hole . . .

Usually the alley rider should move up as the cattle come off the back fence.

3/ . . . until she sees the opportunity to move over and let the extra escape.

4/ Then the team sends its three head toward the gate . . .

5/ . . . and the wing rider gallops toward the gate to call for time.

1/ Here's another team with four head at the top of the arena. The extra cow is making a break here.

2/ She starts to go around the pen, and the rider in the foreground pulls up.

3/ A teammate gallops over to stop a wanted cow from joining the extra . . .

4/ . . . and then pushes the extra by the alley rider, who has moved over to create an escape hole. But this team's problems aren't over.

5/ *When the riders regroup, the wing rider doesn't get in position soon enough, and one cow escapes. One rider will now go after the escapee and try to turn her back.*

Once cattle escape from the pen end of the arena, it can be a real horse race to get them stopped and turned before they reach the herd.

1/ This sequence shows what can happen when the hole man is late. The swing man has brought all three head around the top of the arena . . .

2/ . . . and one cow zooms right by the rider.

3/ The cow on the right stops momentarily, but will probably blast on through the alley since the rider is not in position to stop her.

1/ You don't want it to happen, but sometimes you end up with four head in the pen. This sequence shows a good way to move the extra cow out.

2/ While one rider guards the gate, another rides in and gets between the three wanted cows and the extra.

3/ He gets behind the extra and pushes her out.

4/ And another rider gallops after her to get her across the foul line. In a contest, the judge's flag drops—and time stops—when the extra crosses the foul line.

1/ This team had trouble keeping their three head bunched at the top of the arena. Consequently the wing man was not in position, and these two delinquents saw the opportunity to escape.

2/ Despite efforts by the two riders to block them, the cattle roar by and head for the herd. The rider on the right is trying mightily to get in front of the cows and turn them back.

When a wanted cow escapes from the pen, two riders should go after it.

be called. Normally, two riders will guard the gate while a third goes into the pen, milling the cattle until the extra is pointed at the gate. One of the gate riders will back off, leaving an opening and allowing the extra to go by. Then, one of the penners will haze the cow down the arena and across the foul line for the judge's flag.

Most team penning association rules require that the cows be held in the pen by the team until the extra goes across

the foul line. If there is an escapee before the line judge's flag drops, it's an automatic no-time.

Sometimes, one of the desired cows will escape from the pen with the extra. Two riders should go after it, leaving one to hold the gate. That person should be careful while he does this since he might call for time, by accident. How? He is at the gate, usually with his horse's head inside the pen. It's normal to wave an arm to stop cattle from coming out of the pen; but, if that arm goes up, he's

124

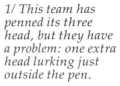

1/ This team has penned its three head, but they have a problem: one extra head lurking just outside the pen.

2/ Two riders wheel their horses and build a fire under them to go after the extra cow.

3/ The third team member guards the gate, and keeps one hand in the air to call for time as soon as the extra is pushed back across the foul line.

1/ Team penners have to contend with all kinds of cattle, including those that are wild and difficult to handle. This cow leaping over the wing was being pushed, but not crowded.

2/ She almost clears the fence, but hangs up momentarily . . .

3/ . . . then crashes to the ground. She was not hurt, and immediately jumped up and headed for the herd. Because there was no contact between the cow and either horse, the team was not called for roughing. The cattle used at this penning contest all tended to be on the wild side.

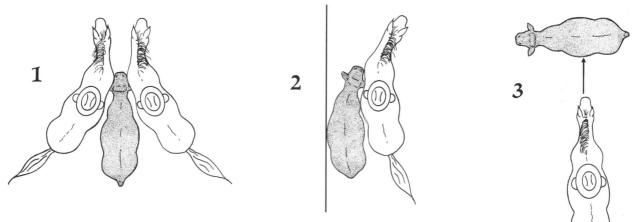

Here are three incidents that can result in a roughing-the-cattle call: 1/ V-ing a cow, 2/ crowding a cow into the fence, and 3/ running into a cow.

called for time with just two head (or one) in the pen. So if his arm goes up, the flag goes down and the time stops.

The escaped cow (or cows) can be brought up on either side of the arena and penned in the normal manner. The person at the gate will move to either the alley or the wing, depending upon which way the cattle are coming from, and his partners will position themselves as needed.

Roughing the cattle. The majority of team pennings have a roughing rule that stipulates that a team can be disqualifed by the judge for any action he feels is unnecessary roughness to the cattle. In some cases, a roughing penalty can result in both a fine and disqualification.

Because roughing is a judgment call by the judge, there are no hard rules on

1/ These two photos show what usually happens when no one guards the gate. This team evidently got two head penned, while one got away. Two riders are after the escapee, but the rider who should be in the gate is AWOL.

exactly what roughing is, but here are several examples that can result in a roughing call:

1/ Running into a cow, or cows. (But if a cow runs into you, that is not roughing.)

2/ V-ing a cow between two horses to stop her.

3/ Pushing a cow so hard that she runs into the fence, or jumps it.

4/ Hitting a cow with your reins, romal, hat, or hands.

Keeping the cattle working. Cattle are sometimes difficult to drive into the pen because they see it as a trap—with no way out. And after they have been penned once or twice, they can become even more difficult to pen.

To remedy this problem, some stock contractors open the back side of the pen and move each bunch of cattle through the pen—before they are settled. As each herd is brought into the arena, riders move the cattle down the wide side (away from the pen) of the arena, bring them around

2/ As a result, the two already penned quickly take advantage of the situation.

the top of the arena, and ease them through the pen. Then they take the cattle back to the herd end of the arena and settle them.

This is done each time a herd is brought back into the arena to be used, or reused. When the cattle know that they can escape from the pen, they are much more likely to run into it.

After cattle have been penned once or twice, they become even more difficult to pen.

12 PUTTING ON A PENNING

As a penning promoter, you must be concerned with a number of things.

YOU OR your organization have decided to put on a team penning, and you are going to run it. How do you put things together for a successful event? A penning just doesn't jump up and happen.

As a penning promoter, you must be concerned with a number of things to put on a successful contest: date, location, cattle, labor, and promotion. Failure to take care of any of these factors limits your chances of putting on a smooth-running penning.

Date. This should be chosen well in advance so you have no conflicting contests within a reasonable driving distance. You want the word out early so penners can plan on attending. That also lets other promoters know that you have that date

filled, and they won't be likely to schedule a conflicting event. Plan on at least 60 days' advance notice, and 90 is better if this is an important contest where there will be lots of money up.

Location. Good facilities are crucial for success. If the arena fence is falling down, the arena poorly lighted, and the ground rocky or hard, you won't have many penners back for your second effort. The following should be considered when shopping for a place to hold your penning.

1/ The arena. Should be well built, well lighted, and with good ground. Does the tractor work (working up and leveling the ground) go with your rental, or is that your responsibility? Make sure you know in advance. Is the location easy to find and

Good facilities are important. The arena should be well built, adequately lighted if the penning will be held at night, and the ground should be in good condition. Too much mud or hard clay will cause horses, as well as cattle, to slip and fall. Note the panels along the fence at the herd end of this arena and along the fence on the far side. They prevent the cattle from being distracted by things going on outside of the arena, and they also prevent the cattle from crashing into the fence.

Pipe panels for the pen should be anchored at each corner to prevent cattle from knocking the panels down. Putting the pen back together takes time, and if it happens repeatedly, can test the patience of contestants and spectators.

on good roads? Penners will travel the back roads to get to a contest, but the easier the trip, the better.

2/ Cattle handling facilities. Are there sufficient holding pens for all the cattle you will be using? Do the pens feed into the arena for easy animal movement? What about loading chutes? Are there water and tanks available for the cattle and is there feed if the animals must be kept overnight? All of these factors must be considered.

3/ Panels, posts, post driver for the pen. The pipe panels should be anchored at each corner of the pen with a steel post. You will also need a post driver and baling wire. Are these available at the arena, or do you have to make separate arrangements? If so, where do you get them and how much will they cost? Make sure you know this before the day of the penning.

4/ Working area for secretary, timers, and announcer. This should be located where the personnel can easily see the arena and the judges, and should be covered, if the arena is outside.

What about a sound system for the announcer? Will it be furnished, is there an electrical outlet so he can hook up his own (if he brings it), or must a long extension cord be run from a generator or outside source?

Where will the judges be located? Is there space in the grandstands, separate stands, or can pickups be backed up

There should be adequate holding pens for the cattle, and each pen should be large enough to hold a set of 30 head. Pens should be sturdy, and have water tanks for the cattle.

against the fence so that chairs can be placed there for them? Flagging a penning is a long day's work, and the judges' comfort is frequently overlooked.

5/ Parking area. Is there plenty of parking for the contestants and their trailers? Is it reasonably close to the arena so they don't have to walk a half-mile back to their horses? And, is there enough room to tie up their mounts?

6/ Concession stand. There must be a place to get food and drinks during the long day/night. Is this a part of your deal with the arena owner, does he operate it, or does an independent contractor do

131

Pens and a chute are helpful for numbering the cattle.

If the penning contest is held in a rodeo arena, the roping chute is ideal for gluing numbers on the cattle. Although some contests are beginning to use numbered belts on the cattle, the majority still use paper numbers glued on each side of the animal. They are made commercially, and are available from several sources.

that? Find out—you could be missing a share of the profits.

7/ Rest rooms. Please, please, please, get plenty, even if you have to rent several portable ones. Make sure they are clean and well supplied with toilet paper.

8/ Insurance. Does the arena operator handle it (have his own) or is it your responsibility? You must be covered in case a spectator or contestant is injured and they sue for damages. The contestants will, of course, sign a release as part of the entry form, but you aren't totally in the clear. Talk with an insurance agent who handles equine event coverage. You might not need insurance, but find out and be sure.

9/ Financial arrangements between you and the arena owner. Is this a flat fee for 24 hours, a fee for the time plus the utilities, a percentage of the gate or number of contestants, or what? Make sure that you know, and have it in writing. If there are any extras, they should be specified, as well as their costs, in the contract. Last-minute surprises have a way of ruining an event.

Cattle. Make sure that you have enough, or limit the number of entries to the number of runs that the cattle can handle. This will depend a lot on the weather and size of the arena. There is no sense in running a herd of yearlings into the ground. If they get tired and won't run, the contestants aren't going to be very understanding. So make sure you have enough cattle. In a sanctioned contest, you need 30 head for every 10 teams, plus a few extra head in case a cow is lame, sick, blind in one eye, etc.

Penning cattle can be obtained from several sources, and they should be contracted for well in advance of your penning. In fact, once the penning date is agreed on, the cattle should be ordered immediately. Specify the number, quality, and the price per head. You should also know if that price includes trucking. If trucking is separate, do you pay for that or does the owner of the cattle? Also, will he number the cattle for you, and if he does, what does that cost? It might be worth it for him to do that job, particularly if he has the facilities at home.

Some individuals make a business of supplying cattle for pennings, cuttings,

The roping chute must be stout, since cattle don't always cooperate. The cattle used at this penning contest gave the numbering crew a hard time because the truck hauling them was delayed 3 hours in delivering them. That didn't allow time for the cattle to settle in their new surroundings before they had to be numbered. Having the contractor number the cattle before he delivers them is a big help.

Dogs—even this flea-sized cow dog chasing a yearling—are taboo at all pennings. Dogs barking from outside the arena fence, or running along the fence, can distract cattle, causing a team to lose control of them.

133

*This is an agreement
that one livestock dealer
uses when supplying
cattle to groups putting
on pennings. It can be
modified as needed.*

**Some feedlots will
rent or lease cattle.**

Sample Agreement to Provide Cattle for a Team Penning Contest

This agreement entered into this _____ day of _____ 19_____.

1. _____ (User) will be conducting a contest at _____ arena in _____ (City), _____ (State), on _____, 19_____. (Give beginning and ending dates inclusive.) This contest will require the following: approximately _____ (loads) totaling _____ (head) of steer or heifer calves weighing a minimum of 400 pounds. _____ (Supplier) warrants and represents that all of the cattle are fresh cattle and to his knowledge have not been used in any cutting contests, practice, or training sessions. The cattle are to be in good general health, with no bad eyes. Upon inspection by a representative of the User, any cattle that do not meet the above requirements shall be excluded from use at the contest and User will not be charged for these cattle. _____ (Supplier) is in the business of buying, owning, and renting cattle for various horse contests and thereby agrees to supply the cattle to User for the _____ (date) through _____ (date) contest with delivery to be made no later than _____ on _____, 19_____, and continuing through _____, 19_____.

2. User agrees to pay to Supplier as compensation for the use of the cattle the sum of $_____ per head times the actual number of head provided by Supplier. Said total sum shall be payable to Supplier upon conclusion of the contest at site of contest. This rate will include all hauling and delivery charges.

3. User shall take possession of the cattle as they are unloaded off of the trucks and shall deliver possession of the cattle to Supplier as they are reloaded onto the trucks. While cattle are in the possession of User, User shall be solely responsible for the care and maintenance of the cattle, and User agrees to exercise reasonable care and maintenance of the cattle while in User's possession. User agrees to provide to the cattle at all times fresh hay and water.

4. In the event any of the cattle die or become injured or crippled while in the possession of the User, then User agrees to pay to Supplier the average cost of such cattle to Supplier, and such animal or animals shall then belong to User. The average cost of the cattle shall not exceed $_____ per head.

_____   _____
Representative of User   Representative of Supplier

_____
Signed this the _____ day of _____, 19_____.

and ropings. They are usually known in the area and can be located by asking around. Before you make the deal, however, talk with other people who have used this individual and find out if he will do what he says. Even a contract won't help you if he shows up with a set of cattle that aren't what you ordered and you have to cancel the contest.

Local auction barn operators might furnish cattle for a penning. Often, these animals are not as uniform as those from a contractor or rancher, but they are cattle. Leasing cattle for a penning can increase the profit on them, especially if they can be put on grass and have time to recoup the weight that will be run off of them. Some feedlots will rent or lease cattle,

The announcer's stand over the bucking chutes makes an ideal location for a penning contest's announcer, secretary, and timers. They can easily see the action, and have protection from weather.

although they are reluctant to do so because cattle will lose weight at a penning.

A local rancher might be willing to provide cattle. But he should be told that the cattle will lose some weight, so he is not surprised when he sees his yearlings being run around and all that weight evaporating.

Labor. This means the people who will be doing the timing, announcing, handling the secretarial chores (entries and paying off), judging, and handling the cattle. If at all possible, hire experienced people; it pays off in the long run with fewer mix-ups. Agree in advance how much you will pay each person for the duration of the penning, and specify what their duties are.

Promotion. The old saying, "Unknown wares find no buyers," applies to putting on a penning. If no one knows that you are holding the event, no one will come. The first move—once the date, time, location, and entry fees have been set—is to tell every penner you know about the upcoming contest. The ol' grapevine works, but that shouldn't be the only promotion that you use.

Attend other pennings and practice sessions. Tell the announcers about your event and get them to announce it over

The judges put in a full day's work, so provide each one with a comfortable chair, and make sure that someone keeps them supplied with hot coffee or cold pop.

135

Fliers produced at quick-print shops are inexpensive and a good way to help promote a penning contest.

the public address system. You can even give that person a typewritten sheet with all the information on it so the message is correct. That helps let people know when and where your penning is.

One technique that works well is to have fliers produced at a local quick-print shop. These should include all the pertinent information, including the divisions of penning offered, the entry fees, and the percentage that goes back in the pot. Include telephone numbers of people who can give more information. These fliers can be stacked on the entry tables at other pennings, distributed by hand, and posted on bulletin boards at area tack and feed stores. You can also put these fliers on car/truck windshields at pennings.

Advertise in your regional team penning association's monthly newsletter. And, if the publication carries a schedule of coming events, ask that your contest be included. This reaches the dedicated penners in your target area.

Since not all team penners might belong to the association, don't forget the area's general horse publications. These reach lots of potential penners and spectators. If they know about the event, they might come out to watch—and will become interested.

Don't forget the Sunday classified section in your local newspaper (in the livestock/events division). Schedule these ads several weeks in advance so people can plan on attending.

To have a successful penning, you have to let as many people as possible know about it as far in advance as possible. Remember, the more who know about the event, the more contestants you will probably have.

Decide, well in advance, what percentage of the entry fees you are going to pay back in awards and what percentages will

go to the go-rounds and the average.
Normally, in contests with small or
medium entry fees, this is 50 percent,
since you have to hold out enough to
cover your operating expenses and leave a
reasonable profit. If there is added money
from sponsors, this will be combined with
the purse to give a bigger pot. Make note
of the added money in your advertising.
The more money in the purse, the more
penners you are likely to have.

Some pennings charge a separate
cattle fee; others include it in the entry
fee. At larger contests, where the entry
fees can range upwards from $100 per
penner ($300 and up per team), usually
only one-third of the entry fee is allocated for operating expenses. The
balance goes into the purse.

Make sure that you have plenty of
office supplies, entry forms, pencils, and
a stapler on hand. Keep track of what
they cost. Running a penning is a business enterprise and you must record
your expenses. Don't forget the numbers
and glue either, unless your cattle
contractor handles this. They are available from several sources and should
conform to the specifications of the
association sanctioning your penning.

Be sure, before the secretary starts taking entries, that there are several pocket
calculators available. Keeping track of the
time and the money gets complicated.

Last, but not least, cross your fingers
and hope that nothing happens to ruin
your day, like bad weather. As we've said
before, penners have good days and bad
and so do promoters.

*This is one type of glue used for numbering
cattle. Ideally, the glue will keep the numbers
on for the duration of the penning, yet will
allow the numbers to be peeled off after the
penning.*

TERMINOLOGY

Team penning talk.

ACROSS THE LINE—Term designating that five or more cattle have gotten across the start/foul line and the team will be given a no-time because of disqualification.

ADDED MONEY—Money added to the purse by the promoter, sponsoring organization, or a business firm. This boosts the total purse above what the entry fees will amount to, and will substantially increase what each team can win.

ALLEY—The 16-foot-wide lane separating one side of the pen from the arena fence.

ALLEY RIDER—Team member who positions himself in the alley and prevents the cattle from escaping past him.

ARENA—The place where a team penning is held.

ARENA DIRECTOR—The person who directs the activities within the arena.

AVERAGE—The total time of each team for two or more go-rounds. The fastest total time for all go-rounds wins the average.

CALL FOR TIME—After the cattle have passed through the pen gate, a team member rides in and raises his/her arm above the shoulder. This signals the flag judge that the team has completed the run. More than one team member can ride into the pen and call for time.

CONTESTANT—Rider entered in the team penning; a competitor.

CONTESTANT REPRESENTATIVE— A contestant elected by the other team penners at a given contest to represent them to the officials.

CORRIENTES—A type of cattle from Mexico, used primarily for roping and bulldogging at rodeos because of their horns.

This team is in danger of being flagged out for having too many cattle across the line (indicated by flag on chute 4). The rider on the gray horse is trying to turn one cow back in front of the chutes, while his partner is turning four others back.

CUT-AND-PEN—A style of penning with a short start/foul line. Because of the tight quarters, the cattle must be handled quietly and cut from the herd, rather than pushed out as in normal penning contests. Once the team has its three head cut out and headed down the arena toward the pen, there is no penalty if the herd drifts across the start/foul line, which is usually only 70 feet from the back fence.

CUTTER—The team member who rides into the herd and separates the designated animals, bringing them out where they can be driven down the arena. The cutter may be a single person who cuts all three cows; or different team members can take turns at the job.

DRIFTER—A single animal that walks out from the herd on its own accord and heads down the arena, usually after the team has finished cutting and is attempting to pen their cattle.

DUCK—A single designated animal that is standing out, away from the herd, when the team rides across the start/foul line and is usually easy to separate. It's a shortened version of sitting duck.

ENTRY FEE—The amount paid by each team to compete in a contest. Normally, a percentage of this entry fee is allocated for operating expenses. The balance is the purse the penners compete for.

EXTRA CATTLE—Any cattle other than a team's designated three head that get across the start/foul line.

FASTBACK—A form of the last go-round at a progressive penning in which the top team competes first, instead of last. Successive teams pen until there is no way that another team can match, or beat, the slowest time that is placing in the average.

FLAGGED OUT—One or more of the judges waving the flag before the team has penned, signaling a rule infraction that has resulted in the team's disqualification.

FLAT-SEAT CUTTER—A style of saddle originally designed for cutting horse riders that has become popular with many penners. The seat has little or no rise in the front, hence the name.

FLORIDAS—A term for crossbred Brahma cattle that originate in Florida or along the Gulf Coast.

GIVING GROUND—When a rider backs off slightly from a cow. There are several reasons for giving ground: 1/ It gives the horse more room to maneuver, thereby giving him better control of the cow; 2/ It reduces pressure on the cow, making her less likely to panic; and 3/ It seems to give the cow confidence and draw her to you, giving you better control.

GO-ROUND—A term used in penning contests (as well as in ropings and rodeos) to indicate a round of competition. A penning can have one, two, or even three go-rounds. All contestants compete in the first go, but not necessarily in the succeeding go-round(s).

HOLE—Another term for the area between the pen and the arena fence.

JACKPOT—A contest where no money is added to the purse. The entire purse is composed of entry fees.

LINE—The start/foul line, indicated by a chalk line across the arena, or by flags or colored wrappings on fence posts on each side of the arena. When a team crosses this line, the stopwatches begin ticking. This is also the same line over which a team must keep extra cattle from crossing.

139

As one rider pushes a cow up the arena, another heads into the herd to sort out the next cow.

LINE JUDGE—The official assigned to the start/foul line. His duties include making sure that the herd has been bunched and is ready for the next team, dropping the flag to start the stopwatches as the team crosses the line, watching how many cattle cross the line, and making decisions regarding roughing of cattle.

LOOK AT A COW—A term applied to a horse when he is really working and showing interest in cattle; i.e., "He will really look at a cow."

ONE-ON-ONE—A penning contest in which a single rider attempts to pen one designated animal with no help.

PEN—The 16 by 24-foot pen, with a 16-foot wing, into which the cattle are driven.

PEN JUDGE—The official assigned to the pen gate. He rules on whether the cattle are in or out of the pen when the contestant calls for time, signals when the run is over, and makes decisions regarding roughing of cattle.

PLACING—Winning some part of the purse in either a go-round or the average; i.e., placing second in the average.

PROGRESSIVE—A type of penning in which only the teams with the fastest time, or only those teams that penned three head, progress to the next go-round.

PROMOTER—The individual or organization putting on the penning . . . furnishing the location, cattle, personnel, and officials.

PUSH—To apply pressure when driving cattle to keep them moving down the arena or through the pen gate.

READ CATTLE—The ability to look at cattle and predict how they are going to handle, and anticipating what they are going to do. For example: "He can really read cattle."

ROUGHING—Bumping, knocking down, or crowding a cow over the fence, or striking or tailing the animal. One or both judges can make a roughing call, which results in a no-time for the team.

RUN—Term for competing one time; i.e., "The team has made its run." Also, spectators sometimes yell, "make a run" as encouragement to a team.

SECRETARY—The person who takes entries, keeps time, and records the results of each contest. A very important person.

140

SETTLE—The process *before* a set of cattle is worked or penned when a single person rides through and around them to accustom the animals to a rider and to encourage them to stay together.

SHORT GO—The last go-round at a progressive penning, when only the top teams compete.

SHOTGUNNING—A style of approaching the herd and cutting when the riders go into the herd one right after another. As soon as the first cutter comes out with his animal, the second one goes in, followed by the third when the second one comes out.

SPOOKY—Nervous, excitable.

STRATEGY—The advance planning of how a team will attempt to work the cattle. Sometimes, but not always, it works out as planned.

SWING RIDER—The rider who swings up and around the cattle at the top of the arena, pushing them towards the pen gate.

TEAM—The three-rider group that enters and competes together at a penning.

TEAM SORTING—A variation of team penning in which only 10 head of cattle are used, numbered from 0 to 9. The team must sort out its cattle in sequence, starting with the number it is given. If it is 5, for example, the team must sort out No. 5 and push her across the start/foul line, then 6, 7, 8, etc. When all of the cattle have been sorted and driven across the line, the herd of 10 is penned in the normal manner.

THIRTY-SECOND WARNING—An announcement from the timekeeper that the team has only 30 seconds left of the 2-minute working period.

TRASH—Slang term for extra cattle picked up by a team. "Trash" must be cut off and put back on the herd side of the foul line before a team can call for time.

TROPHY BUCKLES—Awarded to winning team members at some pennings.

TURN-BACK RIDER—One or more team members who stay out from the herd, "rolling" the cattle back to prevent them from getting out of control and crossing the start/foul line. They help the cutter separate designated animals, push cattle to the back of the arena, and prevent already cut-out cattle from returning to the herd.

TWO MINUTES—The announcement that the designated working time has expired when a team has not penned any cattle.

WANDERER—A single animal that drifts up the arena from the herd after a team has cut out its three head and is attempting to pen them.

WHISTLED OUT—The judge blowing his whistle to signal that a rule has been broken and the team will receive a no-time.

WING—The 16-foot fence panel angled out from one side of the pen gate.

WING RIDER—The penner who positions himself at the end of the wing, functioning as an extension of the wing and hazing the cattle through the pen gate.

WORK—A term covering the description of a team competing once; a run.

PROFILE

Phil Livingston, ready for work as a flag judge at a Texas team penning.

WHEN I told Phil that we needed a profile on him to complete the book, he replied, "Just say that I'm smooth-mouthed and roan-haired." Well, while that might be true, there's a lot more to Phil Livingston than that brief description.

For starters, he is uniquely qualified to write this book because of his strong journalism background, lifelong experience with horses, and many hours spent at team pennings as either a flag judge, watching his wife, Carol, compete, or occasionally competing himself. He's quick to point out, however, that roping is his favorite sport. Since the cow work in team penning is contrary to how a good rope horse rates cattle, Phil doesn't like to use his rope horses for penning.

As a judge sanctioned by both the Southwestern and International team penning associations, Phil has flagged a number of high-dollar pennings. These include the pennings at the Houston and San Antonio livestock shows and rodeos, the SWTPA finals (twice), and the ITPA finals.

As a writer, Phil has sold over 300 free-lance articles since 1961. Those articles have covered horses, horsemen, riding, equipment, livestock, and western art and history. They have been sold to a number of equine and livestock publications, including *Western Horseman* magazine.

Phil also served as horse editor of the *Western Livestock Journal* in 1962. In fact, he credits Aaron Dudley and John Chohlis, for whom he worked at the *WLJ*, for getting him started in equine journalism. From 1982 until '85, Phil served as editor/publisher of the *Paint Horse Journal*.

Phil's writing experience also includes advertising. In fact, he considers himself more of an ad man than a feature writer. Over the years, he has handled the advertising for the Tandy companies (that included Tex Tan Western Leather, Bona Allen Saddlery, and Ryon's Saddle & Ranch Supply), M.L. Leddy & Sons, the

Bank of America agricultural account, Dennis Moreland Enterprises, and, as Phil puts it, "assorted other accounts."

Presently, Phil is self-employed, handling the advertising and public relations for several firms. He works out of his rural home near Weatherford, Tex., where he and Carol keep their horses and several Longhorns given to Carol by Ed Roberts. A long-time friend of the Livingstons, Ed is the executive secretary of the American Paint Horse Association, and also raises Longhorn cattle.

When asked about his early years, Phil

Phil and Carol both enjoy a horse-oriented life-style.

While building a loop, Phil heads for the calves to drag another one to the fire at a branding.

says, "I was an Army brat." His dad, Col. C. E. Livingston, was a career Army man. Consequently, the Livingston family's favorite reading was Rand McNally. Born in El Centro, Calif., Phil attended so many elementary schools, he can't remember which one he graduated from. But he did graduate from junior high school in China, and high school in Toole, Utah. He then attended both Texas A&M and Texas Christian University before graduating from California State Polytechnic College/San Luis Obispo with a degree in animal husbandry.

Phil's interest in horses was triggered by his dad, who was in the old horse cavalry for part of his military career. Says Phil, "I've been crazy about horses ever since I was a little boy, and horses have always been the compelling interest in my life." When the Livingston family was in China, Phil and his dad rode ex-Japanese cavalry horses.

In his younger years, Phil rodeoed in college, in amateur rodeos, and in Rodeo Cowboys Association (now the PRCA) rodeos. Initially, he roped calves, but also rode bulls, and later started team roping. At one rodeo, after a bull dumped Phil

and was intent on mashing him into the landscape, a rodeo clown by the name of Slim Pickens hustled in to turn the bull away. That was before Slim gained Hollywood fame.

Phil's experience in handling cattle started when he was in high school when he cowboyed for several ranches. He has been cowboying ever since, and friends in the ranching business frequently call Phil for his help when they are gathering cattle, branding, sorting, hunting for strays, or doing anything else a-horseback. This work has added considerably to Phil's knowledge of cattle and how to handle them, which proved invaluable when he set out to write this book. He has also run some of his own cattle, and says, "I've lost money with the best of them."

Phil is also an artist of considerable talent. He especially likes to cartoon, and is an inveterate doodler. At any luncheon, dinner, meeting, or conference, he will invariably begin doodling on a napkin or scrap of paper. The doodlings emerge as accurate portrayals of friends, horses, cattle, rodeo action, whatever.

Phil and Carol met while both were students at Texas Christian University. They have three grown children—Jimmy, Kathy, and Linda—and several grandkids. A ballet major in college, Carol taught ballet for some years after she and Phil were married. But she has since "retired" from that profession and works for a publishing company now. She's also hooked on team penning, and spends many evenings and weekends competing with friends at local jackpots. Phil keeps her penning horse tuned up and frequently goes along with her . . . unless there's a team roping jackpot somewhere. That has priority!

—*Pat Close*

Western Horseman Magazine

Colorado Springs, Colorado

The Western Horseman, established in 1936, is the world's leading horse publication. For subscription information and to order other Western Horseman books, contact: Western Horseman, Box 7980, Colorado Springs, CO 80933-7980; 719-633-5524.

Books Published by Western Horseman Inc.

TEAM ROPING by Leo Camarillo
144 pages and 200 photographs covering every aspect of heading and heeling.

REINING by Al Dunning
144 pages and 200 photographs showing how to spin and slide.

CALF ROPING by Roy Cooper
144 pages and 280 photographs covering the how-to of roping and tying.

BARREL RACING by Sharon Camarillo
144 pages and 200 photographs. Tells how to train and compete successfully.

HORSEMAN'S SCRAPBOOK by Randy Steffen
144 pages and 250 illustrations. A collection of popular Handy Hints.

WESTERN HORSEMANSHIP by Richard Shrake
144 pages and 150 photographs. Complete guide to riding western horses.

HEALTH PROBLEMS by Robert M. Miller, D.V.M.
144 pages on management, illness and injuries, lameness, mares and foals, and more.

CUTTING by Leon Harrel
144 pages and 200 photographs. Complete how-to guide on this popular sport.

WESTERN TRAINING by Jack Brainard
With Peter Phinny. 136 pages. Stresses the foundation for western training.

BACON & BEANS by Stella Hughes
136 pages and 200-plus recipes for popular western chow.

STARTING COLTS by Mike Kevil
168 pages and 400 photographs. Step-by-step process in starting colts.

IMPRINT TRAINING by Robert M. Miller, D.V.M.
144 pages and 250 photographs. Learn how to "program" newborn foals.

TEAM PENNING by Phil Livingston
144 pages and 200 photographs. Tells how to compete in this popular family sport.

LEGENDS by Diane C. Simmons
168 pages and 214 photographs. Outstanding early-day Quarter Horse stallions and mares.

NATURAL HORSE-MAN-SHIP by Pat Parelli
224 pages and 275 photographs. Parelli's six keys to a natural horse-human relationship.